Ebenezer

Ebenezer

THE FINAL YEARS OF SCROOGE

DONNA LEE HOWELL

HighWay
A division of Anomalos Publishing House
Crane

HighWay
A division of Anomalos Publishing House, Crane 65633

Printed in the United States of America
08 1
ISBN-10: 0981509185 (paper)

EAN-13: 9780981509181 (paper)

Cover illustration and design by Steve Warner

A CIP catalog record for this book is available from the Library of Congress.

To my family, for their love and support in all my
artistic endeavors, especially my husband,
who kept all the dishes clean so I could write.

Contents

Acknowledgements

A big thank you to Charles Dickens, the original mastermind behind the famous tale, whose writing I could never attempt to equal, and whose story I am honored to have the privilege to continue.

Introduction

First published on December 19, 1843, *A Christmas Carol* became an instant success, resulting in record-breaking sales of over 6,000 copies in its first week, an extreme accomplishment for its time.

The story's popularity played a very important role in completely redefining the significance of Christmas and the primary sentiments associated with the holiday, as it was written during a time of major decline in the old Christmas traditions.

The proud author, Charles John Huffam Dickens, witnessed several events in his life that would later be perceived as similar to the events in *A Christmas Carol*, and these personal connections help bring his story to life.

His family had been comfortably wealthy, and he was well educated at the private William Giles school in Chatham. Their financial prosperity came to an abrupt end, however, when Charles' father, after doling out a great deal too much money entertaining and maintaining his position in society, was sent to Marshalsea debtors' prison. This of course, left Charles in the default position at the age of twelve to provide for the rest of the family, a headcount of six after two siblings died in infancy. He immediately went to work attaching labels to shoe polish at a local factory, submitting himself to the lifestyle of the working class.

Having tasted the existence of the rich and then the poor, every piece of work that he would see through to publication would be unique in its having been written with expertise of both worlds. He saw much death and disease, which was, at the least, a common ground among the destitute inner-city inhabitants. It would not be unusual to assume that he created the character of Tiny Tim as a parallel to someone he'd known first-hand. Additionally, the unabridged version of his book, involving content much darker than our modern movie depictions of the story, suggests that a cultural familiarity with ghosts or the paranormal was also not unusual at that time. It was somewhat after that original dark feel, mastered by Dickens, that I fashioned this sequel.

A Christmas Carol has been noted for at least 11 theater adaptations, 2 operas, 18 films, 5 radio productions, 35 television versions, and countless parodies, standing as one of the most remarkable and renowned stories in history. Yet still, with as much attention as the story has received, there are questions that remain unanswered.

Who exactly were the Ghosts of Christmas Past, Present, and Future, and where did they come from?

Why did the ghosts have an interest in helping a possibly condemned man?

Is it at all realistic to assume that a miserable miser can face these visitors from the other world, change overnight, and then maintain that change?

What happens when London's richest and most dreaded name becomes the richest and most beloved name, resulting in overnight popularity and fame for a person who puts great value on his privacy and time alone?

And one question that has received enormous reflection from the very beginning and today causes massive debate over the Internet: What *was* wrong with Tiny Tim?

The list of questions could likely go on and on perpetually. No author in the world could address every conceivable possibility left open-ended by the original story. However, some of the most mainstream questions have lent me the platform as an author to expand on my own exclusive theories with confidence that any lover of the original book will find this sequel fascinating.

Prologue

The fire cast flickering shadows from the quill across his parchment, lending a pleasant distraction from the ruthless cogwheels churning in his mind. The windows were dark, and no sound could be heard any distance from his front door. It was the peace he had been asking for.

Now that he *had* peace, he could not concentrate.

How could it be that *this* was what he was born to do? The whole idea of it seemed unnatural.

Sighing, he leaned back in his large leather chair. His eyes drifted to the stool where Bob Cratchet used to shiver during long winter days. The un-cushioned, hard, wooden stool now remained almost constantly vacant since the faithful clerk had become a successful doctor.

"Why did I agree to this?"

He should have said no from the beginning. That's what he should have done. Now however, not only was he obligated to finish a great project that he hadn't even started and had already begun to dread, but in order to truly bring the pages to life, he would have to revisit many painful events from his past in great detail. This would not be an easy task, but he had put it off long enough.

Closing his eyes, he allowed his thoughts to wander to two years before. He imagined a scene in which he refused to undergo the project. He could almost taste the freedom. He could just simply move on and never again feel the burdening weight of such a life-altering responsibility!

Ah, but then, he couldn't have moved on just like that.

The idea that he would have let them down would have stuck with him forever and threatened his so-called "freedom" with a constant needling of "what might have been." Yet, that's what it always boiled down to anyway, wasn't it?

What might have been…

All things considered, he believed them anyway. They said this was what he was made for, truly *created* for even.

He trusted them, and the ghosts.

Supposing the only thing he could do now was buckle down and force his hand, he bent forward again in his chair, and pulled the quill from its resting place.

"Alright ol' boy," he said, spinning the feather between his fingers. "The beginning sounds like a good place to start…"

He then twisted the top off his inkwell and dipped…

Chapter One

Still Haunted

The small ghost remained crouched between the solid oak bookshelf and the wall, watching for the anticipated arrival of a second, slightly larger ghost. He should have been here by now. Her small, cold fingers rapped silently against the wall in opposition to the long wait. Taking in a deep breath, she boldly slid one foot closer to the edge of the shelf and peered one eye out into the room.

Elegant draperies and fine china decorated the windows and shelves of the study, and candles burned in different places throughout the room, casting a dim but warm, orange glow over the bindings of hundreds of antique texts and encyclopedias.

Her eyes had for some time now been adjusted to the faint light, and she looked all around for the slightest hint of her friend's location. Nothing. Moments passed and no sound or movement from anywhere. Her hand found the knot at the throat of her cape, and she fumbled it mindlessly. Returning to her original position, she uttered a small moan and crossed her arms at her chest in a pout.

"SHHH! He'll hear you!" came a whisper from a few feet away.

The unexpected reprimand of her companion startled the small ghost, yet she nevertheless felt the relief of his presence. She quickly slid to the edge of the shelf for a second time and looked around the room. Nothing. Her eyes fell on the satin curtain framing the grand window on the opposing wall. The fabric flowed lush and thick down to about two inches above the floor, and there, beneath it, stood two leather shoes, motionless. She had found him. A smile and loud giggle escaped her lips against her will, and she remorsefully clasped a hand to her mouth. Cowering back, she waited for several seconds in the darkest shadow behind the shelf, butterflies whirring about in her stomach wildly. Her heart beat too loudly in her ears for her to attempt to listen for anything else. A whisper of protest and another shushing was barely audible from across the room.

Now she had done it. She was sure of it. She had made a noise and almost assuredly given up their hiding place. What could she do now? She couldn't run without being seen by Bigbad the Pirate!

"What's this?" cried a giant voice from a couple rooms away. "Do I hear the unearthly cackling of a ghost from the world beyond?"

She retreated even farther into the shadows and held her breath.

"Now you've done it, silly!" whispered the voice behind the curtain. "He'll find us for sure!"

A large step pounded the hardwood floor of the study, followed by a second foot being grotesquely dragged behind.

"Oh no," whispered the small ghost. "Bigbad!"

Step.

Drag.

She wiggled as quietly as possible to the floor to watch from under the shelf.

Step.

Drag.

His big pirate feet paused momentarily at the curtain. The urge to warn her friend of his impending capture was almost overbearing. She watched silently, and heard Bigbad the Pirate start to make sniffing sounds.

"Do I smell the life-lacking phantoms that prey upon the living?" the voice boomed, followed by a loud crack on the floor with Bigbad the Pirate's Cane of Entrapment.

"Shivers! Do I feel the chill of ye heartless soul-suckers?"

She pressed herself uncomfortably against the floor and saw the Cane of Entrapment headed for the curtain, and her voice exploded forth from her before she could contain it.

"Marcus! Look out!"

The curtain flew sideways and the more mature ghost emerged scrambling to seek freedom from the Cane.

"Run ye scoundrel!" shouted the giant voice. "Run from the Cane, but ye'll never escape Bigbad! The Cane will trap yer souls! Yarg!"

Marcus scrambled successfully from Bigbad's grasp and turned in time to see the pirate's leg dragging into the carpet at the center of the room. The unexpected contact with the carpet threw his balance, and the huge villain plummeted hard against the floor, causing a thunderous crash. Marcus gasped and rushed toward him.

Within seconds, a tall, medium-build man in a robe hurried in half-shaved, with lathered soap heavily covering the other side of his chin.

The old man on the floor in pirate's clothing moaned and reached for his leg, dropping the cane to the floor beside him. The robed man quickly tightened the fastening around his waist and hurried to the center of the room, offering a hand to the moaning pirate.

"Uncle! What in heaven's name!" He began by lifting one shoulder off the floor carefully. "Marcus! Emily! How did this happen?"

Marcus spoke first. "I was the ghost of the ship, and Uncle Eb was attempting to capture me and trap my spirit in the Cane of Entrapment. I ran out from behind the curtain, and he tripped on the rug!"

"Fred, don't blame the boy," Ebenezer chided loudly, greatly irritated by the inconvenient fall. "It was the poor location of your confounded rug that is the fault of this clumsiness!" Ebenezer's nephew Fred began to help his uncle with a heave from the shoulders onto the velvet settee.

"Uncle, are you alright?"

"No I'm not alright. Can't you see that I'm not alright? Use your eyes while they still work Nephew!" Ebenezer lifted his leg closer to his chest and wailed in pain. "Oh! I will need surgery! I will need pills!"

"Oh Uncle." Fred said stifling a laugh at his uncle's typical overreaction. He glanced about. "Emily! I see you behind the bookshelf! Come out at once and apologize to Uncle Ebenezer!"

No longer enjoying the fantasy of being the Ghost of Pink Christmas, she appeared slowly from behind the shelf. "Sorry Uncle Ebenezer."

Marcus' apology followed.

"Honestly Uncle. A pirate?" Fred chuckled.

"Well my overcoat looked the part, and you know your son's imagination. I had hardly finished eating my supper and Marcus had the game all planned." It was almost as if Ebenezer had forgotten about the pain he was in.

When he suddenly realized they were all watching, he burst out in another cry. "Tend to the knee boy! Oh the knee! It isn't going to heal itself!"

Fred laughed again and shook his head, heading for the closet. Pillows were brought and wedged in around Ebenezer from various angles and a stool was placed at his front. Fred found a towel and patted the lather from his face. Emily began to sing a song she had written on the spot called "It Will Only be a Bruise," causing Marcus to rebel against his four-year-old sister's constant attention-seeking by yelling above her with his own ideas for their next game.

Ebenezer, of course, had to join the noise competition with his own offering of exaggerated wailing. The room, now somewhat chaotic, seemed challenged against its own purpose, for at this moment, the very concept of the word "study" seemed absolutely ludicrous.

Fred appeared in the doorway with a blanket from the master bedroom and hushed the children. Ebenezer had once again been distracted and given up the act for the moment.

"Marcus, Emily, it is your bedtime, and before you begin your nightly protest, know in advance that it will *not* work on me—or your mother—tonight."

Emily pouted and wrapped a finger around a blond bouncy curl as she headed out of the room. Marcus stopped briefly in front of his great-uncle.

"Do you suppose our next game could be in a haunted castle? You could be Jacob Marley!"

Ebenezer did not even attempt to stifle his laugh. "The only game I'll be playing for a while will be a good round of 'Watch the Old Man Limp.'"

Marcus' head dropped sadly as he walked from the room.

The room was quiet now, and Fred rose from the settee and walked calmly toward the wine mobile. He glanced at Ebenezer who nodded once, and returned his focus to the silver-plated bottle opener on the mobile's shiny surface. In moments, the red liquid was pouring into ornate crystal glasses, the sound of rich fermented grapes bouncing against the once again quiet walls of the firelit study. Fred used his dark green robe sleeve to catch the drip from the edge of the bottle as he replaced the cork.

"Well Uncle," Fred began in his usual jovial tone. "What was the game?"

"We were on a haunted ghost ship. Marcus was the head ghost, to which all other ghosts were accountable. I was Bigbad the Pirate, and my mission in the game was to touch and capture all ghosts on board with my Cane, trapping their souls in the other world for all eternity."

"Thus, saving the world from the clutches of something evil no doubt?"

"One ghost at a time."

"Ah!" Fred laughed. "The whole thing was Marcus' idea I suppose?"

"Indeed. Almost too much daydreaming for one small boy."

"Ha! Of course, yes. And Emily?"

"Now Emily," Ebenezer stopped to laugh endearingly. "Emily was the Ghost of Pink Christmas."

"The Ghost of Pink Christmas!" Fred could hardly repeat the words before his head was back, belting out a hearty laugh. Nobody ever knew where Emily's ideas came from or how she thought they related to whatever game they were playing.

So much amusement was gained just by hearing the things those two could come up with. Ebenezer smiled at the thought and silently thanked the ghosts once more for their intervention years before. To think of what he could have become! Lonely, old, angry…

Fred gently offered his uncle a glass and made his way to the chair opposite the settee, taking a seat and crossing one leg over the other. For a moment, they took in the silence and a few deep breaths, both lost in their own independent thoughts. The wine was lush, full bodied, and dry, offering Ebenezer's favorite end to a visit with his family.

Fred's home was a second home to Ebenezer. It was similar to his in wealthy appearance and plentiful in decorations that delighted the eye. Both Fred and his wife Lillian, had taken an interest in various stimulating contraptions, including complicated musical boxes, metal marbles that jumped and moved in circles by perpetual magnet motion, and a sand pendulum. Needless to say, Fred's home was definitely the more entertaining of the two, and appealed to Ebenezer in many ways. He often pondered how much life he had missed sitting alone in the dreary company of himself and the house mice, his home far too large to justify living alone, yet his wealth far too large to justify owning a smaller one. The contradiction of the thought inspired a quiet laugh.

"What is it Uncle?"

"Oh, a silly thought. I've only been thinking of perhaps hanging a few portraits or paintings on my wall at home."

Fred raised an eyebrow inquisitively and stifled a snigger. He found it cute that almost weekly he was surprised beyond his own expectations to see his uncle giddy about discovering yet another feature that "added value to life." It was in such extreme opposition to the hatred for life the miserable miser held in years past. Ebenezer wasn't anything close to the man he was years ago, still the mention of interior decorating was nothing less than humorous.

"What would you hang?"

"That question doubles as the answer to why I haven't pursued it already."

Fred smiled in reply, and his gaze lingered on the candle flickering next to the inactive fireplace, which at this moment offered no contribution to the relaxing ambiance of the study. His lips found the edge of his wineglass, as he thought for a brief moment.

"Uncle Eb?"

"Yes?"

Fred thought for a moment on the delicate execution of his next question, as it was not the first time he had asked, and he feared a repetitious rejection.

"Why…tell me again why you don't make a home here with your family. My children adore you and your games, and Lillian and I would be honored."

Ebenezer didn't have to think of his answer.

"Fred, don't hold offense for me being the kind of man to appreciate my own independence. I may be aging, but I'm only just beginning to live."

"It is because of your new life that I encourage you to spend it with those who care, and enrich it as much as you can!"

Ebenezer knew he would be more of a burden than Fred could anticipate. It was true that Fred knew of the great numbers of people that constantly sought out Ebenezer for spiritual advice and to hear the famous story from the horse's mouth. Yet somehow, Ebenezer couldn't shake the fear that if he moved in with Fred's family, it would be *their* door constantly knocked upon when "the" Mr. Scrooge was nowhere to be found. Fred was offering a home for his uncle. That much was appreciated. But it was clear that he had no idea what amount of privacy his family would be handing over to the public's curiosity upon inviting in a man with such celebrity appeal as Ebenezer.

Truthfully, he had never asked for *this*. He was intensely satisfied every time a letter appeared at his office from an old woman whose faith and love of life had been refreshed because of his testimony. He was elated when wealthy comrades would come in person, having heard his story, and donate generous sums to the vast foundations and charities that he had founded, all the while feeling blessed on their end to hand over the money without a second thought.

Still, he had never imagined the midnight revelations of one fateful night would have such paramount importance to everyone's lives. Massive public appeal to his story erupted overnight, and the word of mouth narrative spread much farther and faster than if he had paid a hundred messengers to telegram it to the surrounding cities. Good had come of it, and for that he was thankful. But he did sometimes yearn for the privacy he had when everyone hated him enough to leave him alone.

Many times he had toyed with the thought of going into hiding, and had gone as far as to begin packing, and then something would happen. He would receive that old woman's letter, or the treasurer of London's orphanages would appear with tears in his eyes and another beautiful story of what Mr. Scrooge's generosity had done for the children. He was helping, all over, and this is what he had promised the ghosts he would do. If he disappeared, people would stop donating, stop contributing, or worse, stop believing. At least a part of him, somehow, needed to be present at all times for his good works to prosper. However, as long as he was still there, seeing, helping, and channeling the largest funds in London, privacy would be his martyr.

Ebenezer sighed, took a drink of his wine, and resigned himself to his place. Fred smiled and also drank.

"In any case, we enjoy your company every time we are graced with it."

Ebenezer released another soft laugh.

"Of course you will say such a thing. If you were to be honest with me and tell me that my company wasn't welcome, you know what would happen."

"I do?"

"Yes." Ebenezer concluded. "I would become a grump."

Fred's laugh was sincere. Ebenezer cackled in response, his teeth stained with wine at the edges. It was a blessing that the possibility of awkwardness in the subject had not become an issue. The moment of disagreement had passed unseen, and they were once again sharing a drink peacefully.

Fred hurried in his nightgown and cap, barefooted down the winding hall, afraid of what he would find when he arrived at the guest bedroom. Another cry was heard. Without hesitation, Fred slammed his hand into the knob and threw the door open, blinking in the dark to find his way. He staggered momentarily as something small nicked his left ear as it flew into the hallway. Raising the candle, he saw that the guest bed was empty. The rest of the room was seemingly empty as well, so he made his way to the other side of the bed to find a wiggling, struggling lump of blanket.

"Uncle!"

Fred was on the floor quick as a flash, candle in one hand, blanket in the other.

"Uncle, stop!"

"NO!" came a muffled answer from the lump.

"Uncle Ebenezer! It's Fred! Wake up! You'll suffocate!"

Fred wanted to help, but also didn't want to receive a metal soap dish in the eye like the last time this happened. Eagerly, he pulled on the blankets, one edge at a time, ready at any second to block an attack, and eventually managed to unveil a breathing hole.

Ebenezer sprang out of his knotted mass, taking in an enormous breath as if it were his first. Slowly, he opened his eyes, and saw his nephew Fred on his knees beside him, peeking out from behind the X his arms were now forming.

"It was summer," Ebenezer began, breathing heavily. "The earth was hot and made my feet burn, and I started dancing."

Fred, seeing that his uncle had come to, lowered his arms and also began to breathe. He sank from his knees to a sitting position on the floor with his legs to his side, exhausted, and nodded for Ebenezer to continue.

"I was dancing to keep my feet cool. They were hot Fred, *so* hot. I looked down, and this large hand came up from the earth and pulled me down. My body sank into the dirt, and slowly I felt the ground caving in on me. The dirt! It was suffocating me! Pulling me farther and farther down until I was at the hot center of the earth, no air, no nothing!"

Fred was there for his uncle, and Ebenezer knew it.

"Nephew," he said at almost a whisper. "What do you think it means?"

Fred reached out and gripped a hot hand in his.

"I think it means..."

"Yes?" Ebenezer urged.

"That you wear one too many pairs of socks at night, and you manage well at wrapping yourself into suffocating knots."

Ebenezer looked at him for several seconds, not saying a word. Then freeing the other hand and pulling some more slack at the neck of his blanket, he cleared his throat.

"You don't believe that it can have meaning?"

Fred felt for his uncle. Ever since the ghostly visitations, his uncle couldn't dream of anything short of muffins and dandelions without waking in a sweat, always wondering if it was supposed to mean something.

"So you threw something at it did you?"

"Yes! Yes I did! How do you know? Does that—does that mean something?" Ebenezer's eyes widened.

"My head narrowly dodged your weapon of choice upon entering the room."

"Oh..."

They looked at one another, and after a few long moments, they each smiled, which slowly lifted the heaviness of the moment.

Fred stood, and offered his uncle a helping hand. Several minutes of untangling commenced, followed by a pat on the back and an exchange of goodnights. As the door to the guest room clicked shut, Fred blew out the candle in his hand and set it on a corner table. The smile on his face faded. Staring down the empty, moonlit hallway, he allowed his weight to tilt against the wall as he ran his fingers intensely through his hair. After rubbing his eyes hard, he then locked them on the back of the door that Ebenezer slept behind. Silently, he sighed.

Chapter Two

A Sense of Foreboding

The breakfast was as good as it had ever been, and his stomach full as usual. His meal with the family couldn't have been more pleasant, beginning the day wonderfully.

It *would* have been the perfect start to the day if it hadn't started to rain. The blasted rain always ruined his mood. Even the lightest sprinkles of that unnecessary, lousy excuse of an addition to the weather pattern annoyed him. Especially when it landed on collections day, in December when it would more than likely freeze into ice.

He already loathed collections day for other reasons. Against his better sense, he had exposed the nice guy within years back and forgiven all debts, and ever since, they took an easy advantage. No matter what landmark change took place to benefit them, in the end, people would be people. Of course, he had treated them so poorly, and he was in much more moral debt to them than they were to him financially. However, enough was enough, and now that everybody was cheery and bright, it was time to be responsible for debts. After the visitations sixteen years before, a few months had gone by, maybe even a year, and then everyone who had once been those with an excuse at the ready before had resumed their supplications.

He didn't want to be the public enemy, or the community dignitary for that matter. He seemingly had to be seen and heard and talked about wherever he went. Not a single day passed in the lives of the other people in town that he hadn't been the subject of at least three conversations. It was indeed a tiring existence, attempting to live up to people's constant expectations, good or bad. It would hopefully not be long however before they would all be ready for him to pass off the duty of collecting to his clerk, and not expect a monthly public appearance.

Besides, with money pouring in from all sides towards Mr. Scrooge's good deeds, it felt as if dealing with the monthly rent of the townspeople had become more of an inconvenience than it was worth.

"Good morning to you, Mr. Scrooge!" a voice interrupted his thoughts.

"Ah yes! Bill Porter! And how are you?"

"Not bad, not bad! How the days have crawled since my last payment…"

Ebenezer stifled a heavy sigh, and offered instead, a cordial smile. Walking toward the man who had just addressed him, he slid through a narrow doorway and into a glass storefront. Slipping off his top hat to knock the loose raindrops over the doormat, he drew in a breath and prepared himself for the excuses. He shook his mid-length white hair free from the shape it had taken under pressure, and loosened his scarves.

"You can only imagine how slow my store has been since Earnest added a few things for the ladies in his inventory next door."

Looking around, the millenary shop did seem to be in the same shape that it was when Ebenezer was there last. Everything from purple riding bonnets to wicker pin-caps with fake fruit to large gardening hats with wide brims secured by shear ribbons. The store was clean and well managed. Bill's reason behind his unspoken extension request seemed valid, and Bill was an honest man.

"I suppose you will be needing an extension?"

Guilt was laden on Bill's soft features.

"Thank you Mr. Scrooge."

"Call me Ebenezer."

"Yes Ebenezer. I will send my son with a check in a week."

Ebenezer nodded and placed his hat atop his head again. Having somewhat ended the conversation, he looked at Bill for a moment. His head was down in shame, and it was evident that he was anxious to be alone, simply because the typical lack of funds were a great humiliation. A twinge of pity twisted in Ebenezer's stomach for the man.

"Bill."

"Yes Ebenezer." He brought his gaze up from the floor.

"What stands in the way of you doing precisely what Earnest did, and expanding and updating your inventory?"

"I…" He scratched the back of his head. "I…"

"Do you mind if I make an observation?" Ebenezer asked politely.

Bill gave a weak and intimidated smile.

"These styles are out of date, and they will not sell if they don't have new appeal. You could also consider an expansion of your market from solely selling hats to clothing, jewelry, or whatever these silly women buy."

Bill felt much smaller at the thought of Ebenezer understanding his own business as well as he, a man who had owned the family store for decades now. Quite honestly, he only owned the shop as a way of income, and because he couldn't bear to part with a business that had been handed down for generations. He never really did personally enjoy his work, and dreamed almost daily of doing something more fulfilling.

"If you do not bring something new, then you are sailing on a punctured ship, and your business will sink. Your payments have been and will be later every month. You cannot afford *not* to invest money in a change, and if you try to continue without a change, you are destined for failure. However…"

Bill shrank during every moment of Ebenezer's advice, but at the word *however*, he looked up once more, hopefully, as if the word itself represented an out to the tremendously depressing truth of his words. He waited for one terribly uncomfortable moment, holding a shaky eye contact.

"Money is what is needed to upgrade to newer, nicer things, and money is precisely what you lack." Ebenezer turned to leave.

"Come by the office for a loan Mr. Porter. My clerk will write up the papers."

He opened the door and, stepping outside, turned to look at the confused, middle-aged man.

"We will make the payments and the interest in your favor, based on revenue in six months from now, and not a single payment due until then."

Bill blinked.

"That is," Ebenezer continued, lifting his chin inquisitively, "if it suits you."

Mr. Porter paused, smiled, and slowly nodded. He looked about the room awkwardly trying to form words of gratitude to fill the silence.

"Good day," Ebenezer said, sparing Bill the responsibility of an obligatory response, and sparing himself the imposition of having to hear it.

Bill was one of the only townspeople Ebenezer had not financially favored at some point. He needed it now, and far be it for Ebenezer not to show him the same business genius he had whipped up at other times for people whose trades, at the time failing miserably, were now very successful. Even though their wealth was nothing compared to Ebenezer's, the more successful the townspeople were in their own businesses, the more money flowed into Ebenezer's office, which he in turn distributed to the most needy orphanages and charities.

Every little bit counted.

Approximately fifty percent of his monies were forwarded to charitable associations and thirty percent to families who could not afford simple groceries or educational supplies. Somewhere in the mix, (Ebenezer's clerk would know) was enough money for him to live quite comfortably and for his clerk to do the same. One could ask how he could maintain happiness on so little a personal budget, always teased by the knowledge of a far greater wealth he could be harvesting for himself. His reply would have been that anyone who equates the comforts of life with money in his pocket will never know the true happiness of a poor man, a theory developed after the visitations of course.

Ebenezer hadn't looked back when he left the shop. He simply continued throughout the miserable weather, destined for the next inevitable excuse.

Why wasn't he working? Why were his eyes always glued to the window? He had no reason to be distracted anymore…

And yet, there he sat, staring, unmoving save for the absent-minded stroking of his fingers down the fringe of his expensive white quill.

Ebenezer knew something had been on the boy's mind lately, and more than just his wife's childbearing. Up until his baby girl's birth, his distractions had been lighthearted. He created happy drumbeats on the edge of his clerk desk with the tips of his fingers and looked around the room constantly. He would occasionally burst out with things like, "Do you think the baby will look more like me or its mother?" He often did look out the window, but his distractions were in anticipation of an exciting event. It was a happy distraction.

This was definitely different.

He looked almost sad sitting there, slowly moving his hand up the quill and back down, wrinkling his eyebrows and swallowing. His usually rosy cheeks appeared thinner, clammier, and shaded. It didn't appear that he had taken his usual interest in the choosing of a wardrobe either, as his slouchy slacks were at least two sizes too big for his bony frame.

"What is it boy?"

Tim cleared his throat and looked down at the paper in front of him, and began writing again. Ebenezer put down his own plume and stood, his knee still throbbing from the previous night's fall, and lightly limped to lean against the boy's desk. He loved the boy, as if he were his own son, and wanted to encourage him to feel comfortable to speak openly.

Slowly he reached out and gently pulled the quill from Tim's skinny, pale hand. He laid it down next to the paper, and smiled.

"What is it boy?"

Tim sighed and fell back in his plush leather chair, and turned his attention to a highly unnecessary, luxurious fire burning in the corner. His face wasn't entirely sad, but had more of a concentrated look, as if he were asked a question that would take a lifetime to answer.

At this rate, it would.

"Boy," began Ebenezer. "If you're going to report for your duty every day with something so well on your mind as to distract you from your work, then at least I believe I am owed an explanation."

He had meant it partially as a joke, but Tim could only afford a feigned smile. Eventually, after several more moments of silence and a heavy sigh, Tim spoke, running his fingers through his clean-cut hair.

"Ebenezer, I am not so tiny anymore."

Ebenezer offered a small laugh. "You are comparatively smaller than other full grown lads Tim. Don't tell me you feel old, I will not stand for it."

"It is only that I have the pressures of life more lately than ever, and that causes me to feel an ongoing sense of a responsibility before unknown to me." He paused, and his eyes narrowed further into the fire as his small arms crossed in front of him. It was getting a bit warm, and the never-ending patter of the rain outside leant an easy disturbance to any train of thought.

"I am truly unaware of its origin, but I…I have a sense of foreboding." He blinked. "My wife is happy, and my daughter is healthy." He paused, obviously attempting to convince himself of contentedness.

"Thanks to your generosity Ebenezer, I have an income much higher than working class, which offers my family stability. My father is a good doctor, and my siblings have all married well and moved to the places where they have always dreamed of living." Tim shook his head.

"These reasons alone would have been more than enough at any other point in time for me to find happiness throughout the day, but as of late…"

Ebenezer stopped looking directly at him and eased himself slowly onto a stool nearby. He propped his sore knee atop the desk and exhaled as he straightened it.

"I honestly don't know. I don't know if I want something to happen, or if I'm afraid of the idea that something *will* happen. I simply don't know."

Ebenezer pinched the area above his knee and once again exhaled, lowering his eyebrows in contemplation of Tim's comments. He was a bit stumped himself as to what to say in support of such vague conversation. He thought hard for the next several passing seconds, and without a proper answer, decided to change the mood a bit.

"This has got to be the most uncomfortable seat a man has ever attempted to sit on. I have numbness in places I forgot I had."

Tim laughed aloud, and turned in his chair to take a look.

"Want to know something sad, Tim Cratchet?" Ebenezer said with some remorse.

"Sad?"

"This was your father's seat as my clerk for years."

Tim shook his head smiling.

"Poor Father."

Ebenezer pulled his foot off the desk and stood again.

"I believe it's the end of the day. Go on, and I'll see you tomorrow."

Tim looked down at his work, and after considering the distracting nature of the day, supposed it would be wise to pick it up in the morning after a good night's rest.

It didn't take him long to have his coat on. Lately, he was always eager to go home and see his four-month-old princess and his wife.

He bid Ebenezer a sincere farewell, and moments later, he was gone. The office was empty and warm. The window allowed a gray light to lie dormant upon the various documents stacked neatly atop the desks. The hardwood floors were highly polished and the room, upon Ebenezer's contemplation, gained the feeling of a dusty, boring, rich person.

He laughed at how appropriate that title was for him.

The door of the office opened suddenly. Ebenezer turned, expecting to see Tim had returned. Instead however, a small boy entered, dressed in extremely wealthy clothing head to toe, healthy pink cheeks, and a bright smile.

The boy approached slowly and politely, and gave a curt bow. Ebenezer was expecting an introduction, but was demanded one instead.

"Are you Mr. Scrooge?"

Instinctively, he moaned aloud at the thought of his day being delayed even a moment by the likes of a small nosy child. It seemed too often that someone would come and want to talk just before the end of the day.

"Yes," snapped Ebenezer irritably. "Who are you?"

"My name is Jack." The boy gave a decisive nod, as if that was literally the only information Ebenezer was after.

"I have heard so much about you." He continued on, regardless of Ebenezer's evident annoyance. "I am in town visiting a relative, and I saw your name on the door. Only moments ago I watched your clerk leave. Is that Bob Cratchet?"

"No," he grumpily replied.

"Oh." The child smiled and took a full circle, taking in the surroundings of the office.

"Is there something I can do for you…Jack?"

Once again the child continued, unable to read the elder's tone. He was completely oblivious to Ebenezer's interest in shooing him away.

"Will you tell me about the ghosts?"

"No. I never saw ghosts; it was all lies and fantasy." Ebenezer waived his hand dismissively. "Now, if you don't mind, my office is closed for the day."

When the boy didn't move other than to smile, he continued. "Where are you from? You have uh—a mother or someone looking for you? You should find them, and release them of their worry of your whereabouts."

"No. My mother is from the neighboring city to the north. She's very ill. She wanted me to come meet a relative and get to know him in case she dies."

The raw candidacies of the boy's statements were a little shocking. Ebenezer was mildly taken off guard. He started to say something, emitted a small breath-like sound, and tilted his head skeptically.

"I will only be in town for a few days, as I will be going back home when mom is better. She told me all about the visionist that lives here in town named Mr. Ebenezer Scrooge, and how you saw ghosts, and I love ghost stories." He smiled with anticipation, and then gave a partial nod, as if prompting Mr. Scrooge to begin.

Ebenezer knew he had never before seen this "Jack" boy, but somehow his manner was familiar. The way he talked and his overall well-to-do appearance appealed to Ebenezer's curiosity.

The door to the office was still open, and he gazed over and above Jack's head to the outside, looking for any possible guardian for the boy. Not seeing anyone, he returned his attention to the child hastily.

"I have had many travel far to hear my testimony, but never one so young as you, lad." He hobbled to where his cane tilted against the desk. "Someone out there is looking for you, and wondering where you've gone."

"Yes." He nodded. "Someone out there also doesn't know anything about me. But they need to."

It was a silly thing to say and did not make the slightest bit of sense to Ebenezer. "Truly," Ebenezer said. "I am sorry for your situation. It's never easy to see a loved one sick." Ebenezer's was the tone of one who knew from experience.

He did have some curiosity about the young visitor, but stopped himself from encouraging the conversation to move forward. The last thing he needed was to have "open to chit-chat with strangers" added to his social resume.

"However, I can't rightly sit in here and tell ghost stories while someone out there has wondered where you've gone off to. You must leave and so must I. I find your continual efforts to remain in my office rude and impertinent. Go back to your…whoever's caring for you."

Jack sighed disappointedly and headed for the door. He turned and bowed again, and, with his hand on the doorknob, mumbled something about somebody needing to be saved and somebody not listening, and then closed the door behind him.

The child arrived uninvited. He was unaccompanied by an adult and didn't even knock upon entering.

Strange.

Ebenezer shrugged off the puzzlement of the unorthodox meeting, and tilted into his cane to gather his things. It was a long day with many frustrations, and he was well ready to be home and in bed for the night.

Chapter Three

I Saw It...

The picture on the mantelpiece...
Margaret was just as beautiful as that, the day she passed on.

How she would have loved this place.

Mrs. Cratchet was always the one who found something wonderful in something ugly, and a purpose and use for something far beyond its glory days.

He remembered how for the most part, his household was always realistic about being poor, and simply thanked God above for what they did have. But she and Tiny Tim often played little imaginary games of living in a big, beautiful house with dreamy high-rise ceilings with chandeliers and stairways to the upper floors, and ornate carvings above every door. In their playing, one would always be the master of the house, and the other took the role of butler or maid. They often dreamed up a house just like this one.

He was the luckiest man in the world when she was there, and his only peace in her unexpected passing was that he knew she was aware of his unending affection for her. Not a day went by when she wasn't sufficiently reminded of her beauty, her laughter, and how those wrinkles at the edge of her mouth were pretty, nothing else.

When she was on her deathbed with that awful fever, his only consolation was that he had no regrets of the way he had lovingly supported and reassured her throughout the years.

Sighing, he placed the picture back down on the mantelpiece. It was evening, and the local flower shop would soon be closing for the night. He only had a few more minutes before he would be off to purchase a bundle for her grave, this being the anniversary of her death, and he had something else he wanted to do.

Behind the closet door in his home office was a large collection of medical supplies. Tape, bandages, muscle ointment, various prescription medicines, leeches, and lollipops lined the shelves. But the small box set atop his patients' files was what he was looking for.

Pulling it down, he gently lifted the wooden lid and pulled from it a bundle of letters, each one without address, sealed with kisses and hand delivered to him in person during various times of his relationship with Margaret. At the bottom of the small box was a plain brown feather, which he very gently slid to the edge. He was always careful with the feather…

He reached for one of his favorites first, a pale yellow parchment without a seal. The creases were becoming delicate and fragile with age, and had begun to tear at the folds. It was written in long feminine letters.

My Dearest Robert,

I can only imagine your feelings right now. It must have taken all the bravery you could muster to approach my father like you did!

I am writing you from the confines of my mother's room. I can hear them discussing the matter as I write. I hope they will approve. After all, it isn't as if you asked for my hand in marriage.

You aren't thinking about marriage are you?

I must go, as I don't have much time.
Here's to a wonderful courtship!
Margaret

"How could I not think about marriage, Margaret?" Bob laughed, tearing up. He had dreamed of it since the moment they met.

Reaching for another, he settled himself on his office chair, and carefully unfolded the thin parchment. It was dated only a few months later.

My Dearest Robert,

Only a week away from the most wonderful day of our lives, and I am so nervous.

Mother and Father still haven't the slightest idea, and my sister is oblivious. The only one I fear is John.

He knows me better than anyone, Robert. He is more than just an older and protective brother. He is my best friend. I feel that he watches my every move, and senses that we have our own plans. So far he has mentioned nothing and remains aloof around my family.

Meanwhile, I have arranged for our tickets to London, and my bags are packed in a secret place.

We will be happy Robert.

Regardless of what opinions my father has, we will be happy, and if never rich in wealth, than forever rich in love.

I believe in us.
Margaret

Bob stared for a moment at her signature. How grateful he was that after all these years, the ink from her quill remained a tangible memory that he could hold in his hand and touch.

His silent moment in memory of his wife came to a sudden halt, as loud shuffling sounded from the front of the house.

"Father! It's Timothy! Let me in!"

He sounded frantic.

Bob laid his precious letters down on the desk and ran quickly through the hall, into the entrance of his large house, and turned the locks on the door. Pulling it open, Tim almost fell forward into the entryway, having only a moment to choose which direction to allow his weight to shift before colliding into the staircase railing. His body folded over the rail as his lungs heaved. Panting, he waved his hand frantically at the door, at which gesture Bob immediately slammed and bolted it.

Slowly, Tim lifted his upper body into an upright position, and accepted his father's strong arm. Making frantic eye contact with him, he limped to the lowest stair and carefully lowered his skinny body. Seeing his father's tremendous concern, he wasted no time.

"I saw…" he began, breathing heavily. "Something…"

Bob crouched at eye level to his son and stared.

"Slow down, Tim. Calm down."

The father in him wanted to shake an answer out of him quickly and see what was going on and whether it meant danger to his son. The doctor in him knew that Tim's body was weak and had little tolerance for this kind of excitement.

"I saw it…behind…the…"

Bob firmly put his hands on his shoulders and looked him in the eye.

"Calm down, son. Be calm. Let's get you to a chair."

Chapter Four

A Return?

Chicken broth warmed over the fire would have to do in the absence of Fred's delicious wine. It was late, and past his bedtime, so anything warm would most likely send him off to sleep without much effort. The night was warm enough, even in December, that the broth wouldn't need to be piping.

His small pots and pans all hung on brass hooks above the fire, ready for such an occasion. Upon lifting the smallest pot, it rattled the others lightly, casting clunky sounds up the chimney.

It wasn't long before a small fire licked the bottom of the pot and sent pleasant waves of salty scents through the room. Ebenezer shifted back in his rocking chair, and watched the flames. Seeing his cane leaned up against the bricks, he smiled, and remembered their game nights before. His knee was a lot less sore now, and most likely need only a few days of walking gently to heal.

His cane…What a funny thing.

He had begun carrying his cane in his early thirties as a social repellant. It was another accessory that, when used correctly, could give him a mean edge. His walk could be sharper and look more peevish if he had to keep up with a cane as well.

When he finally began to truly live, enjoying people's company and inviting those who passed by into conversation, his body had also aged. He now carried a cane because it was necessary.

Ironic.

Leaning closer to the fire, he could see small vapors wafting just above the liquid surface of the broth. Using a hot glove, he removed the pot from where it sat and gently poured its contents into a large ceramic cup and then set the pot on a small metal stool.

He began sipping almost immediately, and pondered the last couple days.

His office was now closed two days a week to allow Tim and himself some time for their own interests. That sort of indulgence was practically unheard of in a city like London, but he could afford it, and mostly for Tim, allowed it to happen despite the inconvenience it put on others in the town.

He had been bored all day, by himself, with nothing to do. He hadn't seen or spoken with anyone since he said goodnight to Tim the night before.

Except for that boy whose name he couldn't remember that randomly showed up without an appointment. But that wasn't all that strange. His mother probably wanted him to meet Ebenezer to encourage him to agree to his cross-city trip. Perhaps she thought his meeting him would help distract him from the reality of her illness.

Looking back, he wished he had spent one more minute of his precious time and escorted the child back to his guardian. Well, there was probably a good chance of seeing the persistent, ghost-story-loving child again during business hours.

The tiles around the fireplace were beautiful, each handmade by a Dutch merchant long ago and portraying a different Bible story. There was Cain and Able, Adam and Eve, one particularly colorful tile portraying Pharaoh's daughters, and many others. But the one he stared at most often was an angelic messenger descending through the air on clouds like feather beds. It was an attractive piece to him for some reason. It was actually the very tile he had been looking at when the late Jacob Marley came through the wall that fateful night. At the time, some part of Ebenezer had hoped the angel would come out of the picture to his aid against his dead friend.

That night changed everything.

He wished he could make Fred understand his uneasiness about living in the same town, let alone the same home as he and his family. Truly he would have loved to move in and enjoy the same rooms, the same meals, the same events. But it would only impose greatly on Fred's family here and now.

Maybe someday.

Ebenezer continued to think about the details of the last few days. It had gone from completely quiet aside from the small crackling fire, to not so quiet. There was a strange rustling just outside the window that, now that he thought about it, had been going on for a minute or so. He paused, and strained his ears to hear. It was just a rustling sound, but not one he had heard before.

Standing, he laid his cup on the stool beside the pot and took a few steps closer to the second-story window. He listened again, and the noise was louder than before, but still seemed a little way off. He started towards the window once again, and heard a distinct thump just under his windowpane, and he froze.

A small scratching sound.

A small creaking sound.

Ebenezer wanted to approach the window and look, but he was frozen and terrified. He felt as if all his blood had drained into his feet.

Another thump.

Heavy, raspy breathing, just outside the glass.

His heart started to pound in his throat and his knees were suddenly weak. He stood motionless, eyes fixed on the glass, and watched, as long pale fingers appeared shaking at the bottom. Ebenezer trembled as the fingers slowly continued to rise, revealing a hand wrapped in bloodstained white bandages. A voice from outside whispered something long and slow, and Ebenezer was terrified beyond his ability to say or ask anything in response.

The hand began shaking, as its long fingers stretched out to grip the glass. Slowly, the fingers slid from the top of the window down, causing a loud, clammy, screeching noise to file into the room. As the fingers reached the bottom, the whispering grew louder, and the name "Scrooge" was clearly audible.

Ebenezer emitted a loud and fearful cry, stumbling back a few steps.

"Scroooooge..."

"Marley?!"

It grew even louder, and the hand curled its knuckles inward and started pounding on the glass.

"Scroooooooooooge..."

Convinced he had done something terrible, and he was now going to pay for his misdeed, Ebenezer blinked tears away and clasped his hands together. He mustered his last ounce of courage.

"Marley, please! Spare me!"

The hand stopped.

"Marley?"

The hand quickly pulled downward and out of sight.

"Marley?"

He blinked, his heart racing, at the now vacant window. He took one step closer, and heard a distinct laughing sound. It wasn't the laughing of something evil. It wasn't the painstaking laughter of a demon or ghost. It sounded like the simple laughter of a teenage boy.

Limping to the window and wrenching it open, Ebenezer threw his head out and peered down at three teenage boys. Two were holding a ladder steady, as the third, plainly dressed outside of a mummy-wrapped arm, climbed down the ladder quickly. All three had burst into laughter, quite happy with themselves for coming just short of causing the old man a heart attack.

Ebenezer couldn't feel his relief above the anger that was bubbling up in every fragment of his body. Enraged, he grabbed the top of the ladder and threw it away from the window.

"Devilish heathens!"

The boy on the ladder fell just a short distance, and stood quickly. He brushed himself off and continued laughing.

"May you suffer your own hauntings!"

Their laughter expanded in response to his threats.

"May you lie in bed every night of your miserable lives afraid of the bumps in the night, and never know peace again!"

They roared with hearty laughter at this, and having folded the ladder once again, ran down the empty street, quickly making only a memory of the whole incident.

Ebenezer shouted after them until the thudding of their heels could no longer be heard. He looked at the edge of the street where they had disappeared for several moments to make sure that they didn't return. He felt numb everywhere. The anger within him against those boys was such that he hadn't felt in years. He generously allowed his mind to wander to a place where those malicious brats were getting what they deserved.

Suddenly something caught his eye to the left.

There, down at the opposite end of the street was a figure standing still. Its long, dark robe covered it completely, its hood draped well over its head, as it stood under the streetlamp, staring. He stared back at it, momentarily expecting it to pull its hood off and be another young kid from the town.

It didn't move.

Ebenezer quickly pulled his head inside and shut the window, falling to his knees against the wall. Grasping his heart over his nightgown, he shook his head and wiped away the beaded sweat from his forehead and eyes. He took a breath in and held it.

Slowly, he crept his upper body to the glass and peered at the end of the street.

Nothing there.

He quickly looked to the other end of the street.

Nothing…

He resumed his heavy breathing, and slid back down to the floor, his heart racing wildly in his chest. His hands and feet were ice cold, despite the rest of his body, which was on fire. Gasping rhythmically for air, he stretched out his sore leg and gave little concern to the fact that one slipper was missing. The inside of his chest itched, causing him to cough.

Slowly, his eyes filled with tears.

The sounds of the room were once again reduced to a crackling fireplace.

Chapter Five

Poor Ebby

Tim awakened to chatter coming from the dining room. He had no idea what time it was, and cared even less.

Stretching and yawning, he tossed the blankets off his legs. It was usual for him to spend the first minute or so of every day sitting at the edge of his bed allowing his eyes and muscles to adjust. As he did so, he listened nonchalantly to the conversation happening a couple rooms away.

"It was dreadful. Simply dreadful."

"Does anybody know who it was exactly?"

"I'm not sure."

It didn't sound like the typical gossip. Tim concentrated, listening hard.

"Poor Ebenezer."

At the mention of "poor Ebenezer," Tim's heart jumped. He stood from his bed and walked quickly into the dining room. His wife, Anna, would have been crying if the news had been anything too serious, and her lack of tears brought him instant relief.

The dining room was moderate, comfortable, and quaint, with a round table surrounded by four chairs and topped with a hand-knitted doily. The window was bright with cheerful morning light pouring onto a tea cozy with a chipped set of rose-painted china glasses. A small teapot had been set in the middle, but it looked untouched, as if it had been offered as a courtesy, but ignored ever since. Their reason for meeting wasn't entirely of a social nature. Even the ladies' dresses were casual brown and navy blue, with very little trim.

His appearance at the doorway gathered the attention of the two. His plump, pretty, brunette wife blinked and raised an eyebrow.

"Timothy, are you well?"

"Yes of course."

"You slept unusually late today."

"Perhaps, my love, I'm just feeling unusually tired today," he said sweetly. He turned his gaze to Fred's wife, and gave a courteous bow.

"Good morning Lillian. Forgive my indecency for appearing in my nightclothes in front of a lady. It is not my typical behavior, but upon hearing your mention of concern for Ebenezer, I thought perhaps getting dressed was not the highest of my priorities this morning."

Lillian nodded and smiled her pink lips sincerely, mindlessly positioning a fallen curl from her golden bun. Tim took a seat and looked at his wife inquisitively.

"Silly boys and their pranks…" Anna said in answer to his expression. She then recounted the incident of the previous evening at the window.

"Surely then, Ebenezer is alright?"

"Of course he is, my love. It will take much more than a child's prank to harm Mr. Scrooge! He's got more bite in him than a cornered snake. My first question was whether the boys were in good health!"

They shared a quick laugh, and then Anna focused her cocoa-brown eyes on Tim, and went on.

"Though unfortunately, the shouting from his window was

loud enough that it has already whispered its way across town, and everybody has their own version of the story."

"Oh no." Tim rested his hands atop his head, and slowly slid them down to his cheeks. "Poor Ebby. What an ordeal..."

"Yes," Lillian concurred. "I believe the last time his name received this much attention was that cheery Christmas morning sixteen years ago when he forgave debts and ran around town with a smile nobody knew his iron face could possess, raving like a madman about ghosts and spirits and second chances."

Tim slid slightly forward on his seat, and his features grew a little more intense.

"Did he say he saw anything real last night? Any ghosts or spirits?"

Anna blinked, confused. "No Timothy dear. It was a prank."

"Yes. I know. I just thought maybe he..." His voice trailed off, and he stared blankly at the floor. Anna reached for his hand.

"Love, are you sure you are well? You look a little pale."

Tim nodded smiling, and turned his attention back to Lillian.

"Do go on. My apologies for interrupting."

"Well, as embarrassing for him as it must be, his name is the first on everyone's lips this morning. When Mrs. Hammond down the street heard a shout in the night, she looked out her window and saw three boys running away from him; all the while he was shouting inappropriate curses at them that they may suffer hauntings tenfold more frightening than his own."

"Can you blame him?" Tim shot out defensively. "It is nothing less than I would have said given his circumstances!"

Neither of the ladies were the slightest bit offended or shocked by Tim's outburst. Both of them nodded quietly, all possessing the same interest in Ebenezer's safety and privacy.

"Fred and I," Lillian continued, "would rather like Uncle Eb to consider our home as his own. Up until last night the answer had always been no. Perhaps now he will reconsider. I suppose we will find out when Fred is done meeting with him. He is there now."

Tim had begun to sweat a little, yet his skin felt cold. His eyes were suddenly very dry. Anna was looking at him with concern.

Promptly and politely, he excused himself from the room using his clothing as a reason to leave.

In his bedroom, he sat back on the edge of the bed and leaned his upper body into the unmade bulk of blankets. His stomach was suddenly nauseous.

"Are you embarrassed?"

"I don't get embarrassed, I have too much pride."

"It is because of the injury to your pride in all of this that brings about my question. Are you embarrassed Uncle?"

"No Fred! Don't be ridiculous! I'm only concerned that by the time the town vultures have had their say, I will be the guilty party in all of this nonsense somehow!"

"Uncle, let them talk." It seemed easy for Fred to say, but his intent was to lessen the anxiety, and that much was appreciable. "Those who truly know you won't think a thing of these silly stories. Those who don't know you will have a hard time holding brainless gossip against you when you have so many good deeds on your record."

Fred thought it a bit useless to continue trying to console him. However, his uncle's slightly limpy pacing was almost unbearable to watch without at least attempting to help.

"Why can't they all just leave me alone?!" Ebenezer spat. "Why in heavens name can't they just find someone else to talk about, pick on, slander, analyze, and stare at?! Must it always be my name and reputation that their slippery tongues have to salivate over?" He continued to pace, all the while stopping here and there to poke about the air with his cane to emphasize his words.

"I didn't sleep at all last night! I practically had a heart attack because of those pathetic brats! While all of London, save for Mrs. Busybody Hammond, were asleep in their beds, I was traipsing up the stairs and down all night, checking every window and rechecking the door! I dozed off once for a moment or two, and dreamed Jacob Marley came down the chimney! I jerked awake so sharply that I pulled a muscle in my neck!"

Fred stifled a small laugh into the freshly pressed ruffle of his dress shirt. He had wondered when he first arrived why a chair had been turned on its side and crammed carelessly into the fireplace. He could only imagine his uncle's moment of rage when this had occurred. The thought had its humorous appeal, but this was definitely not the time. He was sure that the moment of laughter for that detail would be remembered in a few weeks.

"And don't even get me started on the disrespect they showed last night toward issues as real and above their puny brains as spirits and ghosts!"

Fred was intrigued, and lifted his eyes from the buckles of his shoes, back to Ebenezer, who at this point, looked a little cold in his thin, gray nightgown and cap.

"Disrespect against the ghosts, Uncle?"

"Yes! Blasphemy!"

Fred stood a nearby chair to face his own, and gestured toward it. Ebenezer was successfully tempted into resting his knee.

For a moment, Fred allowed time for his uncle, terribly wound up at this point, to breathe. Then he casually threw one leg over the other, and leaning back in his chair, mustered the nerve to ask him a very sensitive question.

"Uncle Ebenezer?"

"What!" Ebenezer was obviously irritated, but it had nothing to do with Fred, and Fred, as usual, didn't take it personally.

"I have always respected your privacy and your secrets."

"Yes."

"May I ask you a question about that night?"

"On with it then." Ebenezer's countenance appeared to calm slightly at the change in conversation.

Fred shifted uneasily. "Do you believe the ghosts were truly ghosts? Angels? Or were they a dream?"

Ebenezer took a minute to catch his breath, and then ran his finger across his bottom lip thoughtfully, gearing up for what could be a very long talk.

"Fred, I am a financial advisor, a banker, a professional money lender, and bill collector. I am not a theologian. The older I get, the harder it is for me to even fathom the truths invisible to this world. If you were to ask me the day after it happened, I would have sworn on every piece of gold in my safe that the spirits were real."

Fred nodded, listening intently.

"I've had a great number of realistic dreams since then. I cannot answer that question indisputably. However, a total transformation such as mine couldn't have taken place without a supernatural intervention of some sort; that I assure you."

Fred sighed, and turned his eyes to the ceiling in thought. Ebenezer cleared his throat, tilted his cane against the chair, and continued.

"There is a fine line between wanting to know the truth, and dabbling in things you should steer clear of in an attempt to find the truth. Some things are just what they are, and should be left alone, and not tampered with. It isn't for me to decide whether God sent those ghosts or if something else reached out to warn me." Ebenezer swept out the wrinkles in his striped nightgown across his knee. "Whether Marley had the ability at all to come to me from another life or not is a question I can't answer, but have pondered many times. It says in the scriptures that the devil himself can appear as an angel of light. Why then, couldn't the Maker of all things then decide to send an angel in mummy's rags and heavy chains to frighten my stubborn old behind back to what is good?"

Fred laughed aloud.

"Ah! I see you have been studying, Uncle!"

"Goodness knows, Fred. I haven't the slightest idea what any of it means!" Ebenezer threw his hands up irritably. "I didn't ask to be visited by ghosts so I could spend the second half of my life defending myself! Old men with canes long ago could see bushes spontaneously combust in the middle of nowhere, and hear voices, and did they share the same ridicule? I don't remember the Israelites shaking and pounding burning bushes outside the windows of *their* tents!"

Fred slapped his knee as he bellowed a laugh. Ebenezer relaxed his expression from aggravation to mild amusement.

"Uncle Eb, I am sure that even the righteous Moses was persecuted in ways that the Good Book does not mention."

Ebenezer nodded meaningfully and offered a giggle. Taking in a deep breath, he shifted his weight back and looked about the room at nothing in particular.

"I do not know the answers Nephew. It changed me for the good. What difference does it make if it was real or a dream?" Ebenezer smiled. "I wish I had started studying all the earlier. Thanks to you, I believe myself to be destined for even more happiness than that which I felt that morning of the change, if that is truly possible."

"Ah it is Uncle! It is possible." Fred nodded, satisfied with the answer that Ebenezer had offered in regards to the ghosts. It seemed a healthy conclusion for one in his place to come to. Rubbing his hand on his chin, he then sighed heavily, and making a clicking noise with his cheek, he once again conjured courage for the question on his mind.

"The mention of happiness…That is another reason that I am here. It would bring my wife, family, and me so much happiness for you to make your home with us."

"Nonsense."

"Uncle Ebenezer," Fred pursued, leaning slightly forward in his chair. "You have mentioned on more than one occasion just this morning that those silly boys almost gave you a heart attack last night. You were alone, and if—"

"Nonsense!" Ebenezer concluded. "I do not wish to discuss this with you again! Nor do I want to entertain any more conversation about last night!"

Without a knock, the front door burst open.

"I heard about last night!" The voice had boomed through the entryway. It was Bob.

Ebenezer moaned as his head fell back on the chair, eyes wide.

"Mr. Scrooge," he shouted from a room away, "I'm so sorry for what you've been through." Bob had for so many years maintained the habit of such a formal greeting, that even to this point in their friendship he could not call Ebenezer by his first name. Closing the door behind him, he marched his lean, awkward body into the next room, nodded a polite acknowledgement to Fred, and proceeded.

"Mr. Scrooge. How…What can I do for you?"

Ebenezer didn't answer. He remained melted into the chair, staring at the ceiling with his arms hanging limply at his side. Bob glanced at Fred hurriedly and helplessly, and Fred just smiled and shook his head.

"Have I come at a bad time?"

Ebenezer closed his eyes and sighed.

"No," Fred said assuredly. "Your timing couldn't have been more cleverly planned. How are you, Bob?"

"I am well." Slightly confused, Bob looked between the two men and cleared his throat.

Ebenezer turned reluctantly to Bob. He sighed again, heavily, and then forced a weak, pitiful smile.

"To be honest, I'm glad it's you," he said. "People have been coming by all morning. Forgive my rudeness. I have been through quite an episode."

Bob smiled warmly, and then glanced about for a chair. Not finding one, he straightened his burgundy velvet vest, and contented himself to stand.

"I trust you are alright?"

"Of course I'm alright! Bunch of rebellious urchins…"

The three of them remained silent for a few moments, each of them reacting to the comment with their own thoughts.

Ebenezer tapped his lips with his fingertips and averted his gaze to the window. A brief image of the night before flashed through his mind. Many things about the boys' prank had him worked up, but it was something else that continued to disturb him.

"The street, under the streetlamp…" He began. The others turned to him attentively.

"I saw something familiar."

"What did you see?" Fred asked curiously. Bob became suddenly very intense. Ebenezer continued to stare out the window. After further contemplation, he shook his head.

"Just something silly that I saw. I'm sure it was solely due to my wild imagination having just been encouraged to wander."

Bob was always a very polite and somewhat timid man. He nervously stepped forward and ran his fingers through his bright red hair. He was struggling hard against his respectful nature not to pursue the subject. He began his own distorted style of pacing and jerked about awkwardly. He cleared his throat once, twice, and annoyingly a third time. It was obvious that he had something on his mind that had been aggravated by Ebenezer's last comments.

Fred raised an eyebrow skeptically.

"Bob, are *you* alright?"

He stopped and looked back at Fred.

"It's just that…" he began without confidence. "Fred, I need to speak with Mr. Scrooge alone. You are my friend, and if it were a secret of my own, I would utter it without hesitation. But I speak on behalf of another, and it concerns something that I must keep between Mr. Scrooge and myself."

Fred was not offended. He quickly stood, now providing a chair for Bob, and bowed.

"If you need anything at all…"

"Yes, thank you," Bob nodded.

Ebenezer gazed curiously at Bob. What could Bob possibly have to say that couldn't be shared in front of Fred?

Fred sincerely offered the two men a kind smile, and gathered his overcoat and hat. Within moments, he was closing the front door behind him.

"Mr. Scrooge," Bob wasted no time. "Tim saw something a couple days ago."

Chapter Six

The Safe

"Good morning Ebenezer!"

It was a voice from the town square. Whose voice, it wasn't in the least bit important at the time.

"Ah, hello Ebenezer!"

"Good day, Mr. Scrooge!"

He maintained his upbeat and steady pace, nodding halfheartedly to the passing people. Everyone was ready for the first day of snow. Little girls had donned their bonnets and boots with fur at the edges, and women smiled proudly just above their brand new knitted scarves. Young boys had already begun tossing crumpled balls of white from behind dumpsters and cart barricades. Markets had brought out their winter merchandise, and steam vapors could be seen from the tops of factories.

Ebenezer was just glad it wasn't raining.

"Morning, Ebenezer!"

"Good morning, Ebenezer!"

With only one thing on his mind at this point, he passed out courtesy waves here and there and made a sharp turn to the left at the next block. He couldn't appear unpleasant, without the fear that his walk would be interrupted by someone's face of concern, nor could he appear pleasant enough to be in the mood for morning banter, for fear someone would stop to chat away precious time. It had always felt like a shorter walk to work until this morning, and now he couldn't seem to get there. His mind was clouded with Bob's words. If only his knee would move faster.

"No, I get to be the Ghost of Christmas Past!"

"You always get to be the Ghost of Christmas Past!"

Ebenezer stopped and turned. Two unsupervised children, a girl and a boy, stood at the edge of a sidewalk, both gripping an off-white sheet. There was a third child patiently waiting next to them wearing a dark gray sheet that had been wrapped with slack at the top to form a hood. A fourth child in an oversized top hat pointed a giant cane toward Ebenezer. The other three promptly turned their heads. They stared at him for a few long seconds. Ebenezer stared back, blinking. It was an odd moment. In the sixteen years of his story's circulation, *this* was a new one.

Uncomfortable, Ebenezer turned to continue the second half of his walk to the office. His reflexes weren't what they once were, but he still managed to come to a sudden halt before running into the waist-high child only inches in front of him. He backed up a step, adjusting his hat, and then looked down at the boy, surprised. The boy just smiled back.

"Jack was your name, right?" Ebenezer asked with extreme irritation of the boy's intrusion.

"Yep! You remember me!" he bellowed excitedly.

Ebenezer took a deliberate step to the side, and continued forward. He was not at all surprised when the boy was instantly, without invitation, walking happily alongside him.

"I was just going to your office to pay you a visit when I saw you a moment ago. Did you know those children?"

"No, but they apparently know me." Ebenezer spoke each syllable more sharply than the last.

Jack was carrying a small wooden spoon. From the handle of the spoon, hung a length of string tied to a small wooden ball. As they walked, he continuously flicked the handle, trying to catch the ball in the bowl of the spoon, causing a click, click.

"How do they know you?"

"The same reason that you apparently do. If you please, I have an agenda."

He continued walking, directing his eyes and body forward in a way that dismissed the child's presence.

Click, click.

"I don't feel that I know you. Fortunately for me, I'm young, and have plenty of time to become better acquainted with you."

"Goody," Ebenezer spat sarcastically.

"Not like you. You're old. Your face is wrinkly, and your knee doesn't bend properly."

Click, click.

Quickening the pace, Ebenezer's nostrils flared and his jaw tightened. The boy at his side kept up with little to no effort.

"How old are you anyway, Mr. Scrooge?"

"I don't know. I lost count when my knee stopped bending properly."

"Seventy-eight?"

Jack had guessed correctly. For the first time since their meeting, Ebenezer looked down at him, allowing direct eye contact. The boy returned the gaze with a big smile, obviously quite proud of himself.

"The mathematics are simple, Mr. Scrooge. My mother told me that you were sixty-two when you were visited by ghosts. That was sixteen years ago."

Click, click.

"How has your mother come to know such personal details?" he asked coldly.

"She knows a lot about you, I guess."

Rounding the last corner, Ebenezer slowed down to climb the seven steps to the sidewalk adjoining his office. He felt a great deal more conscientious of his knee after the boy's comment, and he took the steps one at a time.

"Your story was all she talked about for a while."

Click, click.

"Yes, yes, she and all the rest of London!" Ebenezer had grown beyond irked, and had started to become angry at the boy.

"She was wrong about the ending though. She said it made you like people. I have the feeling you don't like me at all."

"That is the only sensible thing you have said yet."

Click, click, click.

"Give me that infernal plaything!" Ebenezer ripped the child's toy from his hand, accidentally busting the string.

"Hey!" Jack's lips puckered.

"As if your prattling on wasn't offensive enough, you add insult to injury with this intolerable noisemaker!"

Jack stood sadly staring. "People need to be saved, Mr. Scrooge."

Ebenezer scoffed. "Annoying boy, not only do you have a talent for being entirely too forthright in conversation, which is rude, you also have a tendency to say things that make no sense. I find your company tedious. Your guardian probably shares my distaste for you, which provides a worthy excuse for why they never occupy the same space as you."

"I just wish you would talk to me." His small fists were balled against his hips.

"And I just wish that you would leave me alone. Now if only wishes would come true, what a glorious world it would be for both of us." The last step completed, he took a deep breath and listened for Jack's reply.

"Very well then. I will leave you alone."

Ebenezer was only a few steps away from his office. He stopped and stared at the doorway, feeling remorseful for his outburst. He had been very rude himself, and to a child who was only interested in his story because of his mother's interest, a mother who was reportedly ill enough to send him away to another city to be cared for, by an obviously negligent, and so far absent, caretaker. He had definitely not intended to be so ruthless, but he was desperately needed in the office, and the child had horrible timing.

"My apologies." Ebenezer said, looking at the broken toy in his hand. He began to turn. "Perhaps if you come back when..."

Many people were out in the streets and on the sidewalk, but Jack had already gone. Ebenezer looked about for a moment. Feeling even worse, he turned for his office.

Upon entering, he found Bill Porter in merry spirits, a neat stack of papers in one hand, and Tim cordially shaking his other.

"Thank you, Mr. Cratchet." Mr. Porter had been saying as he entered.

"Indeed. Good day to you and the missus."

Ebenezer watched numbly as Bill turned, discovered his arrival, and rambled on for a moment in gratitude for Mr. Scrooge's generosity. He nodded and offered a weak smile, staring beyond Mr. Porter to the back wall. He felt very wrong about his words to young Jack. After a moment, the office door closed.

"Mr. Porter had many new ideas for his millenary shop," Tim said. "I believe he will be smart with your loan."

"I could rightly kick myself!" Ebenezer answered. "If I had a good leg to do it with!"

"What is the matter, Ebenezer?"

"Nothing." He shook his head, and lowered himself into the chair behind his desk.

"I'm an old, cantankerous, crab, that's what." He set aside his cane, and took a deep breath. "Now then Tim. Tell me what's on your mind."

The snow fell against other windows in the town, and collected to form dusty white pillows in the corners, but the window outside the hot office all but seared each snowflake from their very existence.

Inside, the long grandfather clock reminded the room of every second, and its ornate pendulum offered a worthy distraction for the eye. The fire crackled in the corner, as a small log rolled to the back.

Tim's long pale fingers swept across his forehead to remove the beads of sweat that had gathered, and then resumed their stroke upon the quill.

Ebenezer sat with his chin propped on the tip of his cane. The office was already warm when he had arrived, and it now seemed as though the heat intensified with the pressure of the conversation.

"You said the cloak was purple?"

"Yes."

Uncomfortable at this point, Ebenezer shifted back in his chair, and stared at the floor. His hand found a much tighter grip on his cane than was necessary. After a moment, his eyes closed, and with his free hand, he pinched the bridge of his nose and sighed. Tim witnessed this from his own seat, and shifted uneasily.

"Please keep in mind, Ebenezer, that I cannot expect to have this kind of conversation with just anyone. There is only one person in this world other than my father that I feel close enough to share this with."

"Yes." Ebenezer nodded. "I know."

"Besides that, I believe that you are the only one that may shed some light on what I have witnessed."

Ebenezer tilted his cane against the arm of his chair, and calmly rested his hands on his lap.

"You know Tim, this time, I'm glad that it's me," he said peacefully. "Often, I find it an inconvenience that everyone always wants to talk to me." He chuckled suddenly, and slapped his knee. "In the middle of the night, Marilyn Kindle down the street hears a strange sound outside her window, and she comes to me. Daniel Hark's candle blows out all by itself, and he comes to me. Beatrice Rickley's cat is acting funny, and instead of throwing the insufferable animal in the first public trash recepticle in the town square and securing the lid shut with a seventy-five pound weight, sacrificing its wretched carcass to the maggotts, oh yes—she comes to me."

Despite the ire in Ebenezer's words, they had been delivered in calm humor, which was in some ways harder for Tim to digest than if he had flailed about as usual. His tranquil form of conversation came across resigned and weary.

"I feel that there are many people who assume I enjoy being the labeled loony. The town renown," Ebenezer said, and then looked at Tim.

"I wonder… How does anyone expect me to leave my ghosts behind and move on enjoying my life as it should be in my later years? There is no room for retirement. When I sleep at night, that faceless figure in his dark cloak and long white skeletal fingers haunts me still."

Ebenezer's eyes drifted thoughtfully down to his desk.

"Mine are not as lucky as anyone else's nightmares, to find a home in the daylight on the tip of the bedpost. I carry them everywhere. They are always with me. And if for one blessed moment I start to forget them, someone sees something…hears something…"

His cane was in his hand again.

"People wonder why at my age I still pour over my own offices. As long as I busy myself with counting money or calculating investments, I'm not available to recount the events that people are always so anxious about. Do you know what the root word for anxious is?"

"Anxiety?"

"I don't know," he laughed aloud. "It might be the other way around."

Tim folded his arms in front of his chest and smiled at Ebenezer. He had never seen his old friend look so tired. Somehow he was aware that it wasn't just from his midmorning walk to work. He stared for a moment, and watched Ebenezer's knobby, protruding knuckles whiten around the top of his cane. His thin white hair had grown past his shoulders and his usually clean-shaven face had also escaped a blade's attention. His shoulders were slumping more these days, making it appear like his body had somewhat fused into his chair.

Taking a deep breath, Ebenezer smiled endearingly. "So you see? I am glad it is me this time. I am glad that you can open up to me. It is moments like these, and people like you Tiny Tim, that make it all worthwhile."

"Stop referring to me as tiny," Tim smirked.

"Ah, you're skinny as a rail and twice as pale then."

At this, Timothy laughed aloud, which was music to Ebenezer's ears. It had been weeks since a happy noise had emitted from the thin young clerk. The laugh had also inspired a much less intimidating stage for the conversation at hand.

"Now about this strange thing you saw," Ebenezer continued on. "Did it say anything? Whisper anything?"

"No, it was outside; I was inside."

"That doesn't mean anything. You say you were unable to see anything beneath its cloak, correct?"

"Yes."

"Did you see anything resembling a face? Did you see its hands? Anything?"

Tim shook his head. "No. Neither."

"Well...did it in any way, audibly or inaudibly, threaten you?"

"It was a threatening vision in itself, Eb. But whether I felt threatened because it meant me harm or simply because I was afraid, I do not know. It did however seem to be staring directly at me. Somehow, I can't explain it, I sensed it staring...I couldn't see its face or eyes. It was just watching through the window of my living room...It is difficult to find an explanation for it, but it was by far the most frightening thing I have ever seen. Because Anna had taken the baby to visit her sister for the evening, I was alone when it happened, and I simply ran to my father's house, because I did not know where else to go."

"Yes...It is frightening. I know how you feel. Relax in at least knowing that you are not the only one to have felt the pierce of that stare."

"Then you have seen the apparition that I speak of?"

Ebenezer paused for a moment. This was a delicate conversation, and Timothy Cratchet was the last person in the world that Ebenezer would frighten if it was avoidable. Though the reality that someone else had seen it too might offer some relief, Tim might only be more alarmed to learn that the figure Ebenezer saw under the streetlamp the night before had, in fact, matched the same description. It was a chance he didn't want to take. He decided to direct their talk to previously established knowledge of this nature.

"Timothy, you know my story. You know that there was a ghost that indeed matched that description."

Tim felt unsure of Ebenezer's answer. "Yes of course."

"Do you know what other matched description I saw recently?"

Tim's eyes moved toward Ebenezer. "No."

"That of Marley's hand rapping on the window last night, and that hand was attached to a sixteen- or seventeen-year-old prankster. For all we know, your purple cloaked visitor was no more than another idiot from town, setting off to scare you and your family for a good laugh. It's a good thing your wife did not witness it."

"Yes, of course." Tim smiled, a little unsure of himself.

Ebenezer became lost in thought. He couldn't seem to think of anything more that he could say that would be immediately comforting to the boy. It was hard enough telling himself to be calm. Inside, Ebenezer was fearful of Tim's report. What was this thing? Was it a prank? It was more comforting to believe that it was, but according to Tim's description, it seemed to be the same thing he himself had seen…

"I remember when I heard your story for the first time."

Ebenezer looked up from his contemplation, and smiled. "Oh?"

Tim nodded. "I remember distinctly hearing mother and father discuss the subject in the other room when they thought we were sleeping." Tim gave a low chuckle, and laced his fingers together behind his neck.

"Your mother had eyes on the back of her head she did. I'm surprised she didn't know you were listening."

"Ah yes, well, she probably did. Though I doubt she could have cared in light of what had just happened. Not only had father's wages just been more than quadrupled, but she finally had positive and hopeful news about my physical condition. Needless to say, my eavesdropping was more than likely the least of her worries."

Ebenezer nodded in memory of Margaret. "What a woman."

"Yes," Tim agreed. "She was an angelically good lady who always put herself last." Tim took a long, deep breath, and averted his eyes to his inkwell.

"So you were eavesdropping …"

Tim laughed again. "You like a good story, don't you? Yes, I was eavesdropping. I listened to father describe the hooded figure that you had talked about. I was fascinated listening to the story, but I had nightmares for weeks to follow."

"Oh, poor thing."

"I pretended that it didn't bother me when father spoke of the ghosts, because mother was so overprotective, the last thing she needed was one more reason to shelter me from my fears along with everything else. Father was only too eager to share more details of your story, and I wasn't about to stop him."

"If it frightened you, why didn't you want to stop him?"

Tim tilted his head to the side, and squinted, thinking for a moment before answering. "None of us children had seen any life in father for some time," he answered finally. "I almost died that winter, and he was doing all he could to pretend as if it weren't happening, but we all sensed it. I wasn't convinced that I was dying until I had seen that side of him."

Tim brought his hands back down again, and folded them on the desk. "I remember I had written my goodbye letter, just days before the visitations, and laid it under my pillowcase. In my will, I left my crutch to you."

"Dear sweet Tim," Ebenezer's eyebrows were in a knit. "Why in heavens name were you planning to leave your crutch to me?"

Tim smiled and nodded. "It does seem a silly thing now doesn't it?"

"I…I just don't understand."

"Well…I guess my thinking at the time, was that if your cane ever needed replacing, then you wouldn't have to buy a new one."

"But, my dear boy, I had enough money to supply every lame man in the world with three walking sticks each."

"Yes, I know. But your money was the only thing that I thought made you happy. So I figured you might be blessed by my contribution to saving you a few shillings."

For several seconds, Ebenezer did not speak. He was amazed at such a powerful testimony of such kindness from one so small. When he finally spoke, he had to clear his throat first, and swallow hard, to avoid the sentiment that almost made its appearance past his eyelids. "I never knew you cared about my happiness in those days."

Smiling, Tim reached out and began grazing his fingers along the fancy, white, curly-edged plume on his desktop. "In any case, when father found reason at all to prattle on at every meal the way he did after that whole event, there wasn't a soul in the family that would have stopped him."

"Even your mother?" Ebenezer smiled curiously, grateful that the emotions were curbed for now.

"*Especially* mother." Tim laughed. "When he would stop to take a bite, she would scarcely allow him enough time to chew before demanding yet another regaling of your tale. Those were wonderful days in our family."

"Yes well," Ebenezer sensed the slight sadness of Tim's last comment, and acted quickly. "Even more wonderful days lay just ahead. Your healing happened very smoothly."

"Indeed," Tim agreed, allowing his eyes to venture absent-mindedly about the office. "Though it wasn't always easy toward the end. When I had finally started to show true progress, then my mother…"

Ebenezer folded his hands patiently.

"Ebenezer?" Tim suddenly sounded startled.

"What is it boy?" Ebenezer studied Tim's intense stare and followed it to the safe in the corner. The safe was tucked toward the back of the room, where there was often less light. It was made of thick metal with a large padlock.

On either side of the lock were violent scratches stretching several inches. The upper right corner of the safe was home to the largest of many dents, most of which appeared at the edge of the safe's door. Someone had very savagely attempted entry.

Ebenezer quickly reached into his coat and retrieved his keys. Tim rushed to join him.

The mangled lock opened somewhat easily. Ebenezer slid the lock away from the door and opened it. Coins flew out, landing in random places all over the floor.

"What in heaven's name?" Tim said when the clatter had finally quieted. "Who would have done this?"

Tim raced to the door of the office and inspected the outside. He looked all around the edges of the door and peered closely at the keyhole in the doorknob. Ebenezer watched as Tim simply shook his head and shrugged.

Re-entering the office, both men began to look around the room.

Nothing was out of place.

Ebenezer looked back at Tim, who had once again broken out in a sweat. Tim coughed loudly once or twice, and then slowly lowered himself to the floor to collect coins, which was all the safe had contained. Nothing appeared to have been taken.

"It doesn't make sense," Tim said. "Who would hold a key to the office without also holding a key to the safe?"

"Confound it all!" Ebenezer retorted. "How in the name of Jacob Marley should I know?!"

"There wasn't the slightest trace of a break-in from outside."

Ebenezer made his way to the windows. It was clear they hadn't been opened in quite some time, as a heavy layer of dust looked settled and untouched. The chimney seemed a silly notion, and seemed all the more impossible. If an intruder had attempted that route, surely they would have tracked some ash into the room.

"I will contact the authorities." Tim stood, his clerk apron brimming with coins.

"You will do no such thing."

Surprised, Tim blinked, and stared at Ebenezer. "Why not?"

"I have half a mind to do exactly the opposite and contact nobody and for no reason! I am sick to death of this never-ending persecution! One moment spent with the lazy, good-for-nothing, incompetent authorities is one moment ill used! Whoever or whatever wants my money is welcome to it!"

"But Ebenezer, you can't mean—"

"I *do* mean!"

Ebenezer turned his body toward the open door.

"You hear that London?" he shouted. "It's free for the taking! Come fill your greedy pockets with your demise! You want to trade in your life and happiness for an existence of loneliness and misery? I wish you well! And when you're through, you can celebrate by scaring the life out of an old man! Send your brats to my window in ghoulish costumes!"

People had begun gathering outside the office, each one more curious than the next, and at every word shouted, they looked more shocked and appalled.

"Yes, that's right!" he walked toward the door. "Look at the crazy old man! Why is he flying off the handle all of a sudden? Maybe he sees a ghost!"

At this, Ebenezer threw his arms up wailing, and wiggled his fingers at them, making a cynical ghost impression. "Ooooooooooo…"

"I know!" he continued. "Maybe he hasn't had a good night's rest in sixteen years!"

He had reached the door. Everyone was as silent and still as a gathering of statues, horrified. Tim was standing behind him, equally still.

"Maybe it's because the townspeople are a bunch of skinflints and liars, preying upon the hard-earned living of an honest man!"

When Ebenezer slammed the door, it caused several items on the shelves to tremble.

"Bah. Humbug."

Tim cleared his throat.

"Come Tim," Ebenezer said. "We have yet a day's work ahead of us."

Chapter Seven

Tired

The living room was quiet. So peaceful, that the baby's breathing was clearly audible from the bassinet she slept in. The drapes had been drawn back, and the sun reflected off the snow-covered trees just outside in the tiny courtyard, causing a bright light to pour in from the window. Moderate as they lived, the Cratchet's living room had a picturesque quality with their small portraits and hand-stitched heirloom quilts draped here and there.

Tim crept closer to the bassinet and silently peered over the edge.

He smiled.

How could he *not* smile? She was precious.

Anna put her arm around his back and allowed a very quiet sigh. Her lips formed the word "beautiful" to Tim.

Tim nodded, having never seen a prettier baby himself.

He wished he could take some credit for her sweet feminine appearance, but little Margaret, named after his mother, looked much more like Anna than Tim.

Anna was beautiful. She had chocolate-colored hair the exact shade of her eyes, high arching eyebrows, and a long, noble nose that transitioned smoothly into supple, pouting lips. She wasn't skinny like Tim. She had somewhat larger measurements than the average woman, but was in no need of a corset like many women who falsified their curves. She still wore a corset of course, to be above reproach of indecency, but her shape was natural.

Tim looked at his wife for a lengthy minute, drinking in her every contour. There was much to appreciate on the outside, but that wasn't why he fell in love with her. Everything about her was natural. She never attempted to secure a place in the cliques of society. She laughed when she thought something was funny and cried when she felt sad. She picked flowers if she thought they were pretty and indulged in fancy desserts at parties without guilt. She was very much like a little girl sometimes, but Tim knew she was very much a woman at other times.

She was going to make a wonderful mother.

Tim tiptoed around the bassinet and kissed his wife on the lips. His hands grazed down her spine and fell firmly on her hips. He kissed her slowly and sweetly, until they were interrupted by a small sneeze.

It wasn't little Margaret's first sneeze, but it was equally as adorable as the first. It was hard to believe that her next sneeze would be even more cherished…and then it was. Her face momentarily contorted into a potential cry, and then sleep once again pulled her and her delicate infant features into a calm rest.

Tim and Anna shared a silent giggle as their little one resumed her dreaming.

He looked at Anna, and then his little girl.

If anything ever happened to them…

The thought was paralyzing.

Less than thirty feet away he had seen that cloaked figure staring in through their living room window.

In the last few days, his mind flashed back to that moment many times.

He could still see the long, dark purple cloak behind the mist of dusk. Between the trees it stood, in the snow, shadowed by the foggy haze, arms straight at its sides, as still as a stone sculpture, yet very alive.

The memory of it there, ominously lurking about the courtyard, was enough to make anyone's blood run cold.

The question of why it was there or what it wanted was worse.

"Dearest, are you well?" Anna asked just barely above a whisper.

Tim quickly swept his sweaty brow with his sleeve.

"Of course, my love. I am fine."

"Timothy, I am worried. You haven't...been yourself lately."

Tim had already begun shushing her and shaking his head in protest.

"I'm serious. You look pale. You seem to be eating less, and sleeping more. You're distracted much of the time. What is going on?"

"Nothing Anna." He smiled reassuringly. "I am fine. I am truly fine."

This answer seemed to appease the moment.

"Will you go see your father?"

Tim reflected on this thought for a moment. If he agreed, it would at least help her relax for now. Besides, he had been feeling rather lousy lately, and perhaps she was right in suggesting his father's professional input.

"I will go see Father in the morning."

"Thank you dearest."

Anna gazed back down at her lovely newborn daughter.

Tim returned his attention to the courtyard outside.

The new silver teapot whistled loudly, causing Marcus and Emily to plug their ears. Lillian hurried to lift it off its cradled position atop the stove. Once it had quieted, the children continued.

"Hold still Uncle Eb!" Marcus said. "Last time it went up your nose!"

Emily burst into a fit of giggles.

"Well, if you would aim for my mouth instead of my nostril boy, that would be far less likely to happen!"

"Yes. Come now Marcus, your great uncle's mouth is far too big for you to miss! This should be easy!" Fred said laughing.

Lillian watched smiling, as Marcus shut one eye, squinted the other, and with his tongue out in concentration, he steadied the laden spoon in front of his great-uncle's face. After studying the generous piece of frosted sponge cake atop the utensil, Ebenezer opened his mouth skeptically.

By the time Marcus had catapulted what was left on the spoon into Ebenezer's mouth, the entire family was laughing aloud, except for Emily, who was busy counting "frosting trails" on his cheeks. This also sparked a hearty chuckle out the nose from Ebenezer, resulting in a fluffy cake chunk backfire, somehow landing up his forehead and at his hairline.

Fred handed over a fresh cloth, but not until after christening it first with his own happy tears. "Funniest thing I've ever seen!" He said as he slapped his knee.

Ebenezer finally swallowed. "Big mouth maybe, but did you think this was an expandable cave entrance on my face, boy?"

"My turn!" Emily shouted.

"Your turn?" Ebenezer asked, eyes wide. "We're taking turns now?"

She nodded, reaching for the plate.

"No, I am afraid not!" said Ebenezer wiping his face. "One bite each! That was the deal! Your mother's baking is simply too delicious to waste even one more bite on my face, up my nose, in my ear, or wherever else!"

"But," Emily began her protest. "Marcus' clump was almost three times the size of my clump!"

"No," Marcus corrected her in a sing-song tone. "My clump was the same size as your clump, and besides, that's what 'ladies' get when they have to go first."

"But—"

"Emily, Marcus," Fred interrupted. "Stop arguing about clumps. It's time for bed."

The expected whining commenced, followed by an endearing pat on the head for each child from Uncle Ebby.

Once they had finished their dessert, Ebenezer and Fred stacked their dishes together in a neat pile.

"Uncle Ebenezer, are you sure you can't stay for tea or some wine?"

"I thank you, Fred, for the thought, but I must be off. The weather doesn't permit for my usual late visit."

"You're welcome to stay with us for the night Uncle."

"Again, I thank you for the offer, but I must decline. Things have been a bit distracted at the office, and I should be there all the earlier tomorrow."

Fred stood, and offered a hand to Ebenezer.

"Speaking of the office Uncle, how is Tim?"

"He seems a little under the weather lately, but nothing a little time off of his duties won't repair. I have intentions of allowing him a couple days off next week so he can rest."

"That's kind of you."

"I know."

Ebenezer stood and gripped his cane, steadying himself against the edge of the table. After a moment of allowing his blood to circulate, he started toward the door. The hallway felt longer than usual. Ebenezer took each step slowly, and felt his body acclimate to motion again after his restful dinner with the family. Fred, as usual, accompanied him to the door.

At the end of the hallway, Ebenezer stopped, took a deep breath, and spoke very softly.

"The office had an attempted robbery within the last couple of nights."

"Good heavens Uncle! What did they take?"

"Shh! Quiet, you half-wit!" Ebenezer quietly chided, thumping his nephew on the head with his cane. Reflexes brought Fred's hand to his head.

"I don't want to get everyone all worked up!"

"What happened? Who—"

"I don't know," Ebenezer concluded. "We found traces of a vicious attempt to break the safe. Everything was still there. We do not know who."

"Uncle, I'm so sorry…" Fred was at a loss for words. "Is there any way that I may be able to offer my assistance?"

"I haven't the slightest idea. I'm not a detective. I just thought perhaps if I mentioned it you might know something or someone that seemed questionable."

Fred looked down at the floor, cleared his throat and rubbed his head.

"No. I am not employed there. Why would I know anything that would be helpful to you?"

"Good question. 'Why did I waste my time?' is another brilliant question."

Ebenezer continued toward the door. Fred stepped ahead and opened the way for Ebenezer to exit.

"So that's it?" Fred asked surprised. "What are you going to do?"

"Absolutely nothing."

"Nothing?"

"Yes. The thought of doing nothing excites me," he answered sarcastically.

"Wait, what…who—What if it happens again?"

"Either someone out there will become very rich, very quickly, or they will choose another career path based on their lack of skills in the thievery business. Now then, if you don't mind, I will just be on my way. At this rate, you'll be stoking the fire for an hour to regain the heat you've lost."

Fred shook his head in disbelief. He remembered a time when his uncle would have hired a whole army to protect his investments.

"Uncle Eb, don't you care at all?"

Ebenezer stopped halfway out the door and turned. He stared for a moment without an answer. He appeared to be honestly contemplating his answer to that question, without his usual hasty wit.

"I care." He nodded. "I care for the orphanage. I care for the churches, the hospitals, the schools, and the men who will be taken away from their families and forced into workhouses and debtors' prisons."

Ebenezer closed his eyes. He thought about all the promises he had made to the ghosts about helping his fellow man, and being kind, and sharing and caring and many other things. He thought about the moment when he saw daylight for the first time the morning after the visitations. He had felt that nothing on earth could ever compromise his dedication to improving the world every second that he could. He wanted to live, and love, and spread joy.

Just thinking of how things had transpired from what they were then, to what they were now…

"Fred, I am a prisoner, and I have done my time. I want to be released."

Fred stared, unsure of what to say, and equally unsure of what his uncle meant.

"In the light of eternity, the money in my office is the last thing on my mind. I am tired, Fred."

Ebenezer finally opened his eyes. It was a sad sight. His eyes were bloodshot and dry. His lips almost curled downward into a naturally aged frown.

"Do you understand?" Ebenezer asked calmly.

Fred nodded to appease his uncle, even though he was still unsure of Ebenezer's feelings.

"Tired."

They stared at each other again, and after a very puzzling moment for Fred, Ebenezer turned and shouted down the hallway.

"Marcus! Go stoke the fire, lad! Your idiot father has spared you the trouble of having a warm night's sleep!"

Fred didn't react. He was still staring, soaking in the information about the safe.

"Goodnight Fred."

With that, Ebenezer walked away from Fred's home.

Fred closed the door slowly and turned the locks for the evening.

"He's not going to do anything at all..." Fred said to the air. "He's not even going to bring in the authorities...Poor Uncle."

Fred blinked and turned away from the front door.

CHAPTER EIGHT

Jack

The quiet snow-crunch Ebenezer's footsteps caused was almost silent compared to the click his heals usually made against the hard streets. His scarves were pulled tightly, and his long black winter coat was buttoned all the way up. There was a little early evening light left, and he would make it home in time to go to bed early for a change, maybe even before sunset. He could see at a small distance ahead of him, a small boy sitting on the back of a cart, swinging his legs and humming. Upon approach, the boy looked up, made eye contact, and then looked back down at the ground. His leg swinging and his happy humming stopped. Even though his upper-class outfit appeared to be a little too "cigar room" for the young lad altogether, his fancy miniature spats would have looked adorable on the shoes of a happier child.

"Jack?"

The boy looked up again, but said nothing.

"Yes, I thought that was you. I have something for you." The old man reached into his coat pocket, producing the wooden spoon and ball. A fresh knot in the string had been tied, a cheap fix, but at least it made the toy usable.

Jack didn't answer.

"I would uh, like to apologize…" Ebenezer stumbled uncomfortably, "for before. I was uh…"

"Rude?" Jack offered, accepting his toy back.

"Well…" Ebenezer smirked.

"Mean?"

"Alright, alright."

They looked at each other for a brief moment, and then Ebenezer gestured the boy to follow him.

"Walk me home, Jack."

"Oh…okay." Jack hopped down immediately.

"Will you be missed?"

"No. Nobody knows I'm here," the boy said nonchalantly.

"Why am I not surprised?"

Ebenezer continued forward, much slower than before.

"Jack, I'm going to ask you a question, and I want the truth."

"Yessir?"

"Every time I see you, you are alone. You are such a young lad to be allowed to wander the streets by yourself."

"Yessir."

"Have you run away from home?"

"No sir."

Ebenezer looked directly at the child and studied his face. It was usually so easy to see if a child was lying based on their expression.

"You mean to tell me that your mother left you in the care of someone so incomprehensibly negligent that you wander the streets a few hours before dark by yourself?"

"I don't know, Mr. Scrooge."

Ebenezer studied the child for just a moment longer, and then sighed. He seemed honest, which made his situation even sadder.

"Mr. Scrooge?"

"What?"

"Will you tell me your stories?"

"Jack, I do not have time to tell you the stories the way you want to hear them, or the way they deserve to be told." Ebenezer smirked. "However, if it means that I can walk these streets in peace without fear that you will pop out at any moment annoying me about the stories, I will tell you."

"Deal!"

Ebenezer took a very deep breath, rolled his eyes, and then started with a soft smile. He began telling a skeletal version of the story, leaving out details, and patiently dealt with interruptions every few seconds.

"Was it snowing?"

"Uh, no, but it had earlier that day. So, as I was saying, I was on my way home."

"Was anybody acting strange? Like they knew something was about to happen?"

"Listen...I was walking home."

Jack wanted to know everything. He wanted to know exactly what Marley's face looked like on the door knocker, and even asked what his voice sounded like when he whispered Mr. Scrooge's name. He wanted the gory details any young boy would want. He had to interrupt to ask about the part where Jacob Marley shook his chains and whether he was "gross and crusty." He listened intently as Ebenezer explained how Marley had grown so impatient with him that he had undone the binding around his jaw, letting it fall halfway down his chest.

"Wait! What did you do?"

"I was terrified! I didn't do anything!"

"Did he put his jaw back on?"

"Well, yes. I imagine he had to so it wouldn't fall off in the flight."

"Oh! The flight with the phantoms in the sky?"

"Yes."

"Tell me about that!"

With every sentence, Jack's eyes grew larger, and his mouth popped open incredulously at every turn in the story. Ebenezer wasn't one fourth of the way through when he found himself very animatedly narrating the events with detail. He had slowly gone from a mundane and lifeless recital of the events, to speaking excitedly and reenacting each ghost's words in character.

Suddenly he was playing the role of storyteller, and surprisingly enough, he was enjoying it. It was the first time that he had told the story for both his entertainment and the listener's. Jack wasn't searching for spiritual advice or trying to analyze it for some psychological hidden meaning to take back to his patients. Ebenezer didn't have to try to read Jack's expressions to see if he thought the old man was crazy. He could have told the boy that the Ghost of Christmas Past turned into a fish and flopped about the room, and Jack would have believed it. The pure and personal interest that Jack had in the story, for no other reason than to get a thrill, was wonderfully refreshing.

The two continued down the street. They walked very slowly and stopped half a dozen times around each bend. Ebenezer told the whole story just as it happened, and hearing it aloud to a child made it harder to believe it himself. Jack's reactions to the details of the event made it seem like a fairy tale, and somehow made Ebenezer feel as if that was all it was. It was nice to feel the absence of expectation in someone else's company. He had only meant to allow Jack to walk beside him on his walk home, and now found himself standing outside his house visiting with the boy!

Jack had seemed familiar to Ebenezer the first time they met, but not so much as this time. The way the child walked, talked, laughed, smiled…

He reminded Ebenezer of someone, but he couldn't remember whom.

Jack was warm and sincere. He didn't seem at all like the troublesome ragamuffins that had approached him on the streets in the past. He was definitely a curious little tyke, but also had an abnormally keen sense of intelligence and could carry on a conversation with an adult quite well without being confused or intimidated. Additionally, he proved himself a quick learner by keeping his annoying, clicky-spoon toy pocketed during this visit.

Ebenezer liked the boy. He was afraid to become close to Jack because he had remained distanced and calloused for so long, yet he found himself intrigued with the youth...He found himself caring for him.

"So, why did you originally allow money to become so important?"

Ebenezer paused, thought for a moment, and then sighed.

"I was barely older than you, Jack. My father was taken to a debtors' prison."

Jack nodded, and waited for Ebenezer to continue.

"I...I watched them take him away, and he promised he would return someday to take care of my mother and sister and me."

"How long did it take him to come back?"

Ebenezer laughed quietly, and stared down at the ground.

"I never saw him again."

"Oh."

"Shortly after that, I began working with a good friend of mine to support my mother and sister."

"Was that Jacob Marley?"

"No. Marley was later. This was a merry soul named Mr. Fezziwig. I worked very hard for him, and he rewarded me with security for my family."

Ebenezer smiled sadly.

"My mother passed away, followed shortly by my sister."

"They both died?"

"Yes, they did."

"What about at the end of the story? My mother mentioned that you went to have dinner with your family?"

"Ah. That would be my nephew, Fred. My sister bore a child before she died. He is also a merry soul."

He took a deep breath, looked up at the sky, now darkening with the approach of night, and looked back down.

"After my mother and sister died, I recoiled into my own little world. I shut out everybody who cared about me."

"Like your nephew?"

"Yes, like Fred, but also…"

Ebenezer studied the child. Could someone as young as Jack possibly understand anything about the subject of love?

"When the Ghost of Christmas Past took me back to see my mistakes, one of them was Belle."

"A bell?"

"Not a bell, child, a *woman.* Her *name* was Belle."

"Oh."

"I have only ever loved one woman in my life."

"You didn't love your mother or your sister?"

Ebenezer laughed aloud.

"A different kind of love, Jack. Very different."

"The gross kind?"

Ebenezer laughed again, and jokingly poked Jack's belly with his cane.

"You are okay Jack. You're a smart little boy."

Chuckling, he put his cane back on the ground and nodded.

"Yes, the gross kind."

Jack wrinkled his nose.

"And she loved me too."

"Do I really wanna know what happens next?"

"Nothing happened next," Ebenezer easily concluded. "After my mother and sister were gone, I went into business with Marley, and became hateful to everyone and everything that didn't contribute to my pocketbook. I became obsessed and closed off."

His smile faded. "She came to my office and gave me back my ring. Then she simply buttoned up her coat and moved on."

"You didn't try to stop her?"

"No." He looked up the street in thought. "What a fool I was."

"Do you still love her?"

"At times I do. She was the wildest dream of any man. But I can't allow myself to be silly-in-love all the time when I have so much work to do."

Ebenezer looked down at Jack and shook his head.

"You won't understand until you are quite a bit older." Ebenezer smiled, surprised at the lack of awkwardness between them. "I haven't seen her in so many, many years. She was the most beautiful woman in the world, smart and good natured."

"Okay, okay."

"Heh heh. Yes, of all the things I lost, she was one I could not regain."

"I'm sorry, Mr. Scrooge."

"So am I, Jack. I have never had a moment of her memory that I was not sorry."

"So it all started because your father was poor."

"Sort of, yes. Mind you, that does not stand as reasonable justification for the selfish decisions I have made in the past."

"My father's very wealthy. Strong too. I hope that I am just like him when I get older."

Ebenezer looked down curiously.

"Where is your father now, while your mother is so ill?"

"I am not allowed to talk about that." Jack shrugged. "I have very specific instructions I have to follow about the whereabouts of my father. I am not allowed to talk about what he does either."

Ebenezer regarded him strangely.

"I see."

Jack looked up into the sky, and nodded.

"It's getting dark. I should be going, Mr. Scrooge."

"Wait, Jack." Ebenezer furrowed his brow. "Where exactly are you going? Who is staying with you? I cannot just watch you leave again not knowing if you will be safe."

Ebenezer thought it suspicious that the child's mother was strangely ill and his father's identity and vocation was a secret. It wasn't hard to come to the conclusion that the child was mixed up in a dangerous situation.

"I will be safe, Mr. Scrooge. Thank you for spending time telling me your story."

Jack looked down the street, and without another thought, happily waved and skipped away with his mended toy, a click, click, following his every step.

"Jack! Wait!"

Jack stopped momentarily, and smiled.

"I will see you again, Mr. Scrooge! I promise!"

"Jack! Stop! Where are you going?"

"I have to go, Mr. Scrooge! But we will see each other again!"

"Tell me who you are staying with!"

Jack was already running away.

Ebenezer limped after him.

"Jack, come tell me your stories! Tell me about *your* life!"

The small boy, already a distance away turned and shook his head with a smile.

"Another time perhaps! I have to go! Bye!"

Ebenezer was looking around for anyone that could stop the boy, but it was as if everyone chose this moment to turn in for the evening, and the street was vacant. He continued forward, thrusting his feet into the snow ahead.

"Jack, my boy! Stop! Don't disappear on me like this! We need to talk!"

Jack turned once more.

"Oh! Mr Scrooge! Don't forget that he needs saving! Again!"

Ebenezer was far from catching up, breathing heavy, and already beginning to break a sweat.

"What did you say?"

"Bye Mr Scrooge!"

Within seconds, Jack was around the corner and out of sight.

"Blast!" His cane came down hard in the snow.

Chapter Nine

The Letter

Bob removed his white coat and draped it over the back of his chair.

Dr. Cratchet was finished for the day. All he had left to do was make some notes on his patients' files. Sitting, he removed his quill from its stand. He settled himself into a comfortable position, and shuffled a few things about on his desk.

The letters…

He had forgotten all about them when Tim had burst in days earlier.

Smiling, he slid everything else gently out of the way and pulled the letters close. He took the top letter off the pile and pulled the aged paper from within.

Dearest Robert,

I understand your concern for upsetting my father, and I think your concern is honorable. I have considered and reconsidered my father's opposition to our engagement, and I am greatly aware of the influence that his disapproval will have upon the rest of the family. Please have confidence in my understanding of this situation and accept the solidity of my position.

I want to be with you Robert, and that is not up for discussion any longer. My future is my own, and the only person that has the ability to stop that is you. So you have to make a choice.

Tomorrow I will be at the train station as planned. Our tickets to London are one-way, and there's no turning back, as my choice to run will sever the possibility of ever being accepted back. Upon the last boarding call, if I have not seen you, I will return to Mother and Father and a life that is not my own, revolving around a counterfeit happiness and fancy lace. I will live every day under the pressures of a society that I was born into but will never be a part of. I will continue as I used to, with fake smiles and practiced laughter, but in even greater turmoil, because I will have had a small glimpse into a real life—a life with you. The knowledge of what might have been, mixed with knowing how it all ended, will only result in a deeper resentment of my father and this life I am expected to lead.

I love you Robert.

I choose you, regardless of the consequences.

We have the opportunity to lead our lives as only few do, in love, and not in a business arrangement. Money means nothing to me. This is the life we have been dreaming about since the moment we met.

Don't let fear discourage you from allowing our dream to become the most blissful reality.

Yours always,

Margaret

Dr. Cratchet leaned back in his chair, ran his fingers through his wooly red hair, and allowed himself to weep a few soft heaves as he mindlessly undid the cufflinks at his wrists.

If only he could have studied medicine a year earlier, perhaps she could be with him now. He remembered when Mr. Scrooge originally paid for his entry into medical school. At the time, Mr. Scrooge had the idea that his ex-clerk would take as many patients as needed to secure debts, but primarily he would be an in-home doctor for Tiny Tim. It was a wonderful arrangement, and one that to this day, Dr. Cratchet was still abundantly grateful for.

He quickly swept through to his certification in Liverpool, under the instruction of a Dr. Webber. Among all of his students, Dr. Webber smiled most upon Robert Cratchet, who was the most eager to learn and had the most precious motives behind achieving his goals speedily. In almost no time at all, Dr. Webber pulled Bob out of the class and continued his tutelage in private.

Bob received his certificate months earlier than his colleagues, and with much higher achievement records. Dr. Webber was a good-natured man, a smart and efficient teacher, and made himself available as a continual reference, indefinitely, should the new Dr. Cratchet have any questions.

While Bob was away in training, Mr. Scrooge personally escorted Tim, along with Mrs. Cratchet, to the most trusted of local specialists to oversee Tim's improvements.

Immediately following Dr. Cratchet's return home, he nurtured and cared for Tiny Tim personally, and placed him on a myriad of pricey vitamins and strict diets to build his strength. His son's health greatly improved, and it looked as if there was a remarkable reverse in what was thought to be permanent damage to the boy's nervous system.

Shortly thereafter, therapeutic muscle-building sessions were established and crammed into a busy schedule between meals and pills and exercise. Every moment of every hour of every day was focused on the boy's health.

When Margaret fell ill, Dr. Cratchet never saw it coming.

Why couldn't she have spoken up earlier? Why did she wait until her fever had taken hold? Didn't she know that he could have helped them both at the same time and also tended to the sick in town?

But he knew her own reasoning well enough to know that if she thought her own sickness would result in a lack of progress with her son, she would remain quiet. She always did whatever had to be done to protect the boy, both because of her maternal nature and because of other reasons that Bob would someday share with Tim. He knew she didn't mean to neglect herself to the point of fatality, but her own health and comfort had always come last.

Still, forgiving himself for letting her get so sick was asking a lot.

The next letter was almost begging to be read, as it was one of his favorites. It landmarked the beginning of a new life.

My Dearest Robert,

I cannot begin to describe what it felt like to spend all morning at the station searching for your silly, worn-out tailcoat through the crowd! At the sight of you, my heart leaped as it did when we first kissed!

I knew you would come to me.

Oh how sweet you look sleeping. The sight of you here turns this gray, placid train car into a lavish, rich velvet chariot!

You poor sleepy thing…

I have been thinking, Robert. After we arrive in London and locate a church to be wed, what will we do then? So much of my mind has been focused on our controversial union that it is only just now occurring to me what we will soon be up against.

Your words of caution are ringing in my ears much louder now, as if it were the first time I had heard them. I would be lying to say that I am not afraid, but the happiness I feel sharing my life with you greatly outweighs any fear of the unknown.

I choose for now to simply smile, and enjoy the scenery—*you* of course!

Yours in love,

Margaret

The happiest moments of their lives quickly followed the writing of this letter. Their love was unlike any other in books or stories, and they cherished the small things between them that most happily wedded couples were entirely oblivious to, as the next letter would read. Their lives were very soon filled with the pitter-patter of little red-headed Cratchets, and giggles and laughter that would bring warmth and color to even the drabbest of London's cold flats.

Dr. Cratchet read one letter after another. Mrs. Cratchet displayed a very healthy disposition through the years. However, there life together had not been without struggles.

Dearest Husband,

I must share something with you that I have not mentioned as of yet. I wanted to remain silent of my concerns until I was sure.

I do not fret for what we lack, my love. I know that your new employer will see fit to increase your shillings per week when you have undoubtedly impressed him with your diligence. Though, perhaps if you could find an appropriate time, might you mention to him that your wife is with child?

Forgive me my impertinence, Robert. I know it is a wicked thing to prey upon someone's generosity, but you *do* work hard, and I fear that this child may be different for us.

Do not ask me how I know. I suppose that it falls into my motherly responsibility to know. However, a deep emotional warning finds me every other second during the day, and I feel an almost unnatural movement inside me.

It is as if this unborn knows something, or senses something.

I don't say this to concern you. I don't know for sure what it is I'm feeling. However, I have not grown to the same size that I did with our other children. I look down at my stomach, and I feel terrified! Robert, don't you remember what it was like with the rest? Now when I see my reflection, I see the wanting of at least five more inches to compare with the others.

I wish you could be here with me. Yet I understand why your new employer thinks that for your first several months you should work into the evening if you are to become a successful clerk.

When you think to, please show appreciation for me, and from all of us, that he has allowed you a place in his office. He will ever be dear to our hearts.

Sweet Robert, my body is weary. I must sleep. I'm sure you will find this letter safely when you arrive home.

Forever yours through everything,

Margaret

And yet another, without envelope, without signature, written in her most passionately lonely moment—

My Dearest Robert,

How can he continue day after day, week after week, month after month to keep you there, away from your life at home and your family? I'm trying to be understanding of his interests as your employer, but he doesn't *own* you!

You MUST stand up to him, dearest! You cannot allow your children to be told for even another day that their father is not coming home again because he is working late into the night. For that matter, my love, you cannot continue to tell your wife that she must carry a child alone, all the while attempting to manage and maintain four other Cratchets, as well behaved as they may be! I know you have a respect for Mr. Scrooge, but your family needs you.

I would never question your intent. And forgive me, as I hate to complain. But I feel alone. Robert, for the first time in our blessed, splendid marriage, I feel alone!

I'm worried. The baby did not move all morning. I am due at any moment to deliver this little life into the world, and it's perfectly still. I don't know what to do.

Please stand up to that good-for-nothing employer of yours, or God forgive me Robert, I will.

I feel sick, Robert. I feel pain. Why does my

The final incomplete question on the page added an unfriendly ping to the guilt that already begun stirring again in Bob's gut. He had never forgiven himself for not being there the night of Tiny Tim's birth.

He remembered vividly the moment that he was awakened by the midwife, and drawn from his office where he had worked all night, on the warm morning of July fifth.

Mrs. Cratchet had given birth to Timothy alone.

By the time the midwife had arrived, the birthing was over. The baby was beautiful, but much smaller than he should have been.

Bob arrived in hysterics. After satisfying his immediate concern for the child's health, he cautiously handed the baby to the midwife and flew to his wife's side. She was as pale as the linens she laid upon, and sweat beaded all over every inch of her body. Shortness of breath and pure exasperation had given her usual gentle face a short-tempered look. She had faced the entire test without him. He wouldn't blame her for any grudge she held.

The small child was quickly brought to the bed in wrappings.

That moment was life-changing for Bob. He stood there, tears streaming down his cheeks, and watched as his wife consoled the sweet, quiet little life in her arms. Her eyelids drooped heavily.

"Timothy…Such a tiny little thing." she said. "Tiny little Tim."

Dr. Cratchet cleared his throat, and blinked away tears.

"Oh Margaret," he said softly. "I never deserved your forgiveness." Gently folding away the page, he tucked it neatly to the back of the stack and looked once more to the pile of letters.

"Yet, you gave it to me without my having to ask." Smiling, he turned his eyes to her picture, one of the few he had left over the years.

"Strongest woman who ever lived."

Bob read one after another, the precious years chronicled by the late love of his life. The years that followed…The never-ending financial exertion...The sweet young boy that would lose much of his childhood to the treacherous trials of his weak body...The constant struggle with Robert's vile employer...The unchanging judgment and ridicule from shallow townspeople due to their lack of nice things...The tiny family member whose health caused fear of death, yet the love of life in all of them...The historical day when the miserable employer changed forever...And the happiest and closest family throughout it all...

The letters that remembered.

When he had finally reached the last one, he thought long and hard before making his move.

Was it time that Tim knew? If Margaret were alive, would she have told him already? How would Tim handle knowing the truth?

Bob nervously tapped his fingers on the yellowed parchment.

Margaret's genteel personality had been mirrored by her penmanship in the other letters. This one was different. Her previous scripted right-slant style was replaced with a shaky scribble. Bob was surprised it was even readable, having been written only hours before she died.

He knew that he was to deliver this letter to Tim at just the right time, as Margaret had said. It might have sounded like nonsense to anyone else, but Robert knew her better than anyone. He knew she could sense things nobody else could.

His thoughts drifted. It had been around a week since Anna had encouraged Tim to go see his father for medical reasons. Tim had claimed just a few days before that, that he had seen a figure in his yard. Of course, there was no direct link between these things...

These were unusual events for certain. Still, was it enough to justify the momentous unveiling of the lifelong secret?

Perhaps it was.

"Goodnight Margaret. Until next year."

The box was gently returned to its resting place as it had been before, save for one letter missing. Bob tucked the plain brown feather and the delicate letter carefully into his business coat and draped the coat once again over the back of his chair.

Chapter Ten

The Trip

Tim pulled his quilt up to his neck and tucked it behind his shoulders, his hands then making their way down to pinch it around the underside of his knees.

The train car was frigid, and just the sight of the falling snow outside lent an additional chill to Tim's thin bones. His mug of fine German tea had already gone cold, and the peddler pushing her cart of food and drink up and down the length of the train would be at least another half an hour before her return.

Tim never liked travelling alone. His wife was good at studying the train's routes and scheduled stops. He didn't like having to strategize over it himself. However, if his memory served him correctly, Dr. Webber's establishment was just a few blocks down from the specialty office supply store that Ebenezer had often sent him to for purchasing the finely pressed parchment and better quality ink. At least he thought that's where he had seen it before…

It was a chance he was willing to take, and hopefully he wouldn't bump into any acquaintances, though that also was a chance he had to be willing to take.

The door of his train car slowly slid sideways, and a lady passenger entered. She glanced down at her ticket once and then returned her gaze to the seat opposite Tim. She looked equally as chilly as Tim, which comforted him.

He thought about the story he had given everyone back home. Guilty butterflies fluttered about his midsection when he remembered how he told his wife he was off to replenish the empty supply cabinets above the safe. Strangely, he felt even worse hiding the supplies from Ebenezer, all the while the old man scratching his head and blaming the sudden disappearance on his senile tendencies. "Oh go buy some more, boy!" he had said. "Confound it all! Even my inkwell has to be mysterious!" Tim felt much remorse remembering how it had thoroughly ruined Ebenezer's day to think he had been losing his mind.

Nevertheless, his dishonest plan had worked, and he was now immediately headed for the specialist. Peace of mind was the only thing he was after, and once he had it, he could calmly explain to everyone else why his lie was unavoidable, and why he felt that honesty would have only caused unnecessary panic.

Panic, Tim thought, was the last thing Ebenezer needed these days. His recently increased paranoia and sense of weariness didn't seem to be a healthy invitation for further alarm. Not to mention this small obsession he had adopted within the last week of searching for this "Jack" boy. He had moved his heavy wooden desk closer to the door, and upon every noise that may have been a child, Ebenezer jumped and craned his neck to the window or limped quickly to the door.

"He promised we would see each other again," he kept repeating. "Bah! Promises are a humbug!"

Tim felt for him but hadn't the slightest idea of how to helpfully intervene. He had never even heard of this person before a few days previous, when Ebenezer seemed disturbed by their meeting. The boy had apparently said something strange right before he ran off, about…rescuing somebody or something. Ever since, Ebenezer was, needless to say, distracted. Tim had no idea what to think about this addition to Ebenezer's endless mysteries. If it wasn't one thing, it was another, and it had seemingly always been that way.

Ebenezer was a good friend though, and always there in any way he could be.

Fumbling with the quilt at its edges, Tim managed to find a hole that had been letting in the chill of the train car. He tucked and wiggled and shivered and took in a deep breath before turning his gaze away from the snowy window to the plush purple upholstery of the firmly mounted bench. Why was it so cold? Did they think the passengers would be exercising on their trip?

On the other hand, he had felt very cold most of the time lately.

Hopefully his father's old professor would be able to shed some light on some of the strange things that he had felt and seen as of late. Not that he lacked confidence in his father's professional opinion, however, he was too familiar with Tim's medical history, and may have been less inclined to catch new symptoms.

The most frightening of all recent symptoms was his apparition sightings. If in fact they were apparitions. For all he knew, they could have been hallucinations, or possibly exaggerations of truth. He could have seen an old woman with a dark purple riding hood boarding the train earlier, and somehow in his mind, the vision of that cloaked figure was all he could remember.

He had been one of the first to board, and just barely caught sight of it staring right at him. It appeared motionless, amongst a crowd of people, right before Tim's snow boot rested on the first step. He stood for several seconds squinting back at the figure, until the gentleman behind him had deterred his focus. He vaguely heard a question of his well-being. His first instinct was to point to the figure and see if the gentleman was able to see it too, but by the time he returned his gaze to the crowd, it was gone. Hesitating only a moment longer, he offered the gentleman a kind nod, and then cautiously proceeded onto the train.

He couldn't even be sure this time that he had seen anything at all.

That didn't stop the chills though.

"Brrr…It's cold in here," the lady on the opposite seat said.

"No…" Tim answered, shaking his head.

"It's freezing."

Chapter Eleven

Footsteps

A low whistle of the far-off northern-bound train bounced off the icy, brick buildings of the empty street. The usually gently swaying flags and awnings of the local businesses were strangely still. The snow had let up after a few fresh white layers, creating a soft crunch at every footstep. Darkness had begun to fall like an ominous blanket over the city. Although it was getting later by the moment, it wasn't yet late enough to explain the lack of lit candles in the black windows of the houses lining the street.

Ebenezer walked with his chin up, his eyes stern and unaffected by the eeriness of his surroundings, but inside his mind raced wildly with frightening thoughts. He was determined against his own fear to face the walk home from the office. How stupid he was to have waited until dusk to head home.

But what choice did he have, with as much as he had to accomplish by himself that day? After all, several days without a clerk undoubtedly added up to more than a day's work.

Dismissing his fears with a decisive breath, he continued onward.

It could not be described as a pleasant evening. Something didn't seem right. However, he knew that Tim would be home safe with his family for a few days after he'd returned from restocking his supplies, and the thought of it brought him comfort.

Ah, Tim. What to do with Tim…His mind was almost always drifting somewhere at work as of late anyway. What little work he did accomplish was not without mistake.

What was it that Tim actually saw? Was there any chance that it would reappear while Tim was enjoying his days off of work?

The thought brought chills.

No. Don't think about that now.

But what of Jack? What a strange and unfitting puzzle piece to add to these other recent developments. He had thought of everything he could short of reporting this child to the authorities, and still had not come to any conclusions.

Would he live out the rest of his days wondering if he was even more negligent than the boy's supposed caretaker? Or would others have also reacted to the boy similarly? What could he have done differently that could have—

Ebenezer froze, outwardly pretending to be deep in thought, and listened for the footsteps behind him to continue.

They did not.

Perhaps he had imagined them.

Clearing his throat aloud with fabricated confidence, he continued his walk away from the office.

Moments later, he froze again, this time unconcerned with his brave presentation, and turned sharply around. The footsteps sounded closer, yet nothing was there.

He didn't budge, squinting through the twilight in attempt to see anyone, or anything, moving. Slowly, he turned forward and stared for a moment straight ahead at the street.

Still nothing.

As soon as he attempted another step, a snow-crunching sound was heard somewhere close.

"Humbug! I know you're there whoever you are! Come out and face me you cowardly ninny!"

Nothing.

"I'm not afraid!" He continued to listen as his eyes darted around. "Young hooligans think you'll frighten me?"

After several long seconds with no movement or answer, he slowly and skeptically resumed his walk. Instantly the footsteps behind him moved also, growing closer to him with each step.

Ebenezer began a pitiful run, looking behind him at every possible opportunity. Within seconds, his old and out of shape body had already strained itself, and he was gasping for air. Between the crunching of snow under his feet, the desperate breaths, and his heart suddenly pounding in his head, he had lost hope of hearing anything behind him.

It was getting darker by the second.

He was only fifty yards away from the next street.

"Help! Somebody help me!"

He no longer cared if someone hearing him thought he was a lunatic. Nor did he care what had been following him. A sudden, unexplainable fear gripped his chest, and he threw his body forward, one awkward lunge after another.

"Please! Somebody!"

He could see the snow fling behind him on the white street as he glanced back again. His eyes stung in the cold as he raced on ahead.

The corner was approaching, and he quickly stepped up to the sidewalk and healed a sharp turn to cut directly into the next street. He looked quickly in both directions. To his great dismay, this street appeared to be deserted as well. Again, despite its early evening hour, candles in the upper windows were already extinguished. Not a soul occupied any of the businesses on ground level, and anybody that had planned to travel on foot tonight had either done so already or hadn't left yet. The street was empty, as if something had been planned to happen now, and that was a very frightening thought.

Ebenezer made a snap decision to take a right. As he turned, he took one last glance down the street toward his office.

Something in the distance shuffled out of sight and into the shadows of a building.

He stared.

He held his breath.

He squinted.

He collected the courage to remain there.

This time, he had locked his eyes on the general area of the movement, and knowing where to look, he stood firm.

Again, something moved, but within the shadows of the building, it appeared only as a dark fog, bent low in a crouch.

"Show yourself, you wretch!" Ebenezer spat courageously, his heart pounding like a gavel against a thin sheet of metal.

Whatever it was, whoever it was, it had begun moving now, quickly moving toward him.

"Who are you?" he demanded, feeling his knees weaken with every millisecond.

It did not answer.

Long, easy breaths emitted from it as if it knew it had won, and Ebenezer was simply a bug to be squashed.

It grew steadily closer.

"SOMEBODY!" Ebenezer shouted, staring into the shadows.

It was approaching fast.

"Somebody help! I need help!" he shouted, glancing up and down both sides of the street.

The silhouette in the darkness started to slow down and gradually stood up to its full height. It wasn't abnormally tall, and as it began to take shape, Ebenezer could see that its movements were smooth and graceful.

All Ebenezer needed to know was that it was slowing down. He was off again, down the street, limping away from his predator. Knowing the true danger of his situation now, he began to cry. It was no longer a question of whether or not this thing was human or ghost or anything else.

It was simply out to get him, and he didn't stand a chance.

He fought against the urge to allow his weak knees to collapse from beneath him. A small pain started to grow in his chest.

Was this it?

Had he not changed at all? Had the dark spirits finally had enough of his evil deeds? Would he go to that dark place and take up the chains that he forged during life, just to spend an eternity among the misery of the phantoms he had seen in the sky on his journey with Jacob Marley?

Without warning, a loose brick in the road gripped the front of his shoe. He went down with a heavy thud.

What happened next was a blur.

Ebenezer looked up just in time to see a silky dark purple cloak ripple its way into view from behind the building at the corner. Time seemed to slow to a crawl, as this thing slowly emerged and walked several steps closer. It turned its shape toward Ebenezer and stood, its intimidating form facing the small fragile man on the ground, cowering helpless in the snow.

Ebenezer shrank in fear.

"Who are you?"

The figure, now in full view, paused at its prey.

"Are you a ghost?"

Ebenezer studied its appearance. Its long sleeves produced no sign of hands. Its hood was too dark to see inside.

The figure did not move.

"Will you not speak to me!?"

Facing the inevitable end of the chase, Ebenezer whimpered, and tightened the grip on his cane. Almost instinctively, he mustered the strength to quietly utter five small words.

"God in heaven…help me…"

The figure continued to stand there, staring ominously, almost damningly…Finally, a small line of silver glittered from the figure's sleeve. As a short blade eased into view, the figure shifted into forward motion again.

Suddenly, it stopped.

Its purple hood swiveled quickly to focus on something just over Ebenezer's shoulder.

A faint light fell softly upon the purple cloak. Quickly, the light grew brighter, but still, nowhere nearly bright enough to trace a shape within the hood.

Had his small desperate prayer worked?

Was there really light cast on the street, or was it a product of his exhausted, feeble mind?

Its long sleeve lifted in front of its dark face, and it backed up slowly. As the light grew slightly brighter, the figure's movements grew faster. It turned and scampered away, no longer smooth and effortless. The figure almost appeared to Ebenezer to be frightened as it fled from view around the corner.

After gathering the courage to look, Ebenezer craned his neck to see the godsend whose timing could only be described as divine.

Behind the glass of the storefront just one door up from where Ebenezer lay, Bill Porter was already hard at work in his shop clothing and apron, scattering boxes about and folding what looked like new fancy fabrics. He moved quickly and excitedly about the area, racing in and out of view of the street. His lamp glowed luminously just within the door.

"M…Mr. Porter!"

Ebenezer hadn't even thought about the damage the fall had done to his old body until that moment. The knee that he had injured while playing with his niece and nephew was beginning to throb again, and his hip was beginning to ache.

"Mr. Porter, I'm outside!"

The lamp was hoisted immediately, as Bill peered under his fingers through the glass. He looked about the street, and his eyes finally met with Ebenezer, who at this point was waving his cane in response.

Bill quickly unlocked the door and opened it, looking again out into the street.

"Mr. Scrooge, sir?"

"Mr. Porter, come quickly! Help me up!"

"What in heavens!"

He was quickly at his side, resting his lamp on a lump of snow.

"Just help me up! We don't have time for explanations! It is not safe out here!"

At this, Bill moved quickly.

Bill's entire body felt strong next to his own, as Ebenezer rested his weight against him. He swept up the lamp in his free hand, and painstakingly limped towards the store. About a minute later, Bill gently lowered his acquaintance onto a bench just inside, and then scrambled to lock the door behind them. He took the lamp and slowly walked the length of the storefront, peering out of the glass in every direction, while Ebenezer choked and gasped for breath.

Seeing nothing, Bill eventually gave up trying, and without demanding any immediate answers, went immediately to searching the stockroom for his most powerful brandy. Emerging a moment later with a glass and bottle, he rushed to Ebenezer's side and started to pour.

Typically brandy was not Ebenezer's choice of drink, however this time, he found himself almost guzzling. He breathed for a moment after the glass was gone, and then set it down beside himself on the bench.

He was lost in wonder.

Somehow, unexpectedly, it was over. He had escaped death.

Now, he was sitting after hours in a storefront with a man he hardly knew, who stared at him with such concern that one would have thought they had been best friends for quite some time.

"Mr. Scrooge?"

He didn't answer.

His breathing had finally started to slow, and he sat, staring straight ahead.

"Mr. Scrooge, sir?"

Bill patiently stood and scooted a stool closer to the old man, and sat. He hadn't the slightest idea what had just happened, or why Mr. Scrooge was found late in the evening on the street in the snow. Nor did he know what was going through his mind as he continued to stare straight ahead, not answering. Nevertheless, he was determined to remain calm despite his apprehension.

Ebenezer blinked the sting out of his tired eyes. He was bewildered by all that had transpired since he had left his office. Was it a human or ghost? How long had it been following him? Was it watching him now? Was it in fact the same thing Tim had seen? Would it be there always, lurking in the shadows of London, awaiting its old, withered prey?

So many questions raced through his head at lightning speed. He couldn't think or focus. This was too much for him to handle! He was simply too old for this!

Ebenezer thought for a moment about the gleaming blade that lowered from the sleeve of his predator, and he gasped aloud.

Bill placed his hand on Ebenezer's shoulder. It was obvious to him that he had been through more out there than a simple trip and fall. Ebenezer was terrified and shaky.

"Mr. Scrooge?" he tried again patiently.

Ebenezer continued to reflect on his experience. That would have been it. Whoever or whatever that thing was had intended to end his life. It was a miracle that he was still alive. Maybe he shouldn't be. Perhaps it was a ghost that was sent to take him to his chains once and for all.

"Mr. Scrooge…are you ill?"

Perhaps it was his time.

"Mr. Scrooge?"

Perhaps it was the ghost of so long ago, come back to fulfill his promise of delivering Ebenezer to the afterlife. Ebenezer had thought he was doing good for mankind. He had a list a mile long of ways he had channeled his strengths and abilities for those less fortunate. He loved his family and made himself a better man!

"Mr. Scrooge, I'm sending for the doctor."

Was he being punished for allowing Jack to disappear? Was his role in Jack's life supposed to be more? Was he deaf to his calling for Jack? Was that why he had been pursued? Or, even worse, did this dreadful creature have something to do with why Jack was suddenly nowhere to be found?!

"Ebenezer Scrooge, I'm sending for the doctor!"

"No… That won't be necessary."

Bill stopped and relaxed himself back on the stool.

"Mr. Scrooge?"

"No…I don't need a doctor."

Ebenezer thought of the small child. He remembered his happy nature. He thought of the boy inviting himself into his office and without introduction, asking about ghosts. He remembered how cruelly he had dismissed the child, even breaking his toy, and guilt hit his stomach like a brick. He thought about how the boy had promised they would meet again, and how he had not seen him since. He thought about a small helpless child like Jack lost in London with that *thing* wandering around…

"Oh…my God, my God…" Ebenezer shook his head. "My God, be with him."

Bill, starting to grow afraid, reached for the brandy himself.

"Uh, Mr. Scrooge, sir…Please…What is going on?"

Suddenly Ebenezer remembered the moment that the light appeared faintly on the cloaked figure from behind his own shoulder. He looked up, and his eyes met with Bill's.

"Mr. Porter," he said with his eyebrows raised high on his forehead.

"Yes, Mr. Scrooge?"

"What are you doing here?"

"Mr. Scrooge, I think you've had quite a tumble. I've been here the whole time. I helped you inside remember?"

"No." Ebenezer shook his head frustrated. "I mean at this time of evening, hours after your store has closed! Why are you here?"

"Oh." Bill nodded. "Now that you mention it, it is a coincidence that I was. I received the shipment off the cart yesterday for my store's new inventory. I had been closed all day, and thought perhaps with diligence, I could be open for business tomorrow."

Bill tapped his fingers on his glass.

"I was at home a while ago, and felt the urge to come back and organize. I was only here for a few moments when I heard a shout from outside." He paused awkwardly. "Mr. Scrooge, what has happened?"

Ebenezer looked at him, and suddenly realized he had a choice to make. He thought about the last time he was open about his visitations, and how it had changed the entire course of his life. He thought about the immediate responsibility that he would have inflicted upon himself personally, and his family, if word got out that he had met with another ghost. If he told the truth, his story would spread like a brush fire, and by morning he would be held accountable to recount the event to every nosy neighbor once again, just like he was before. He and his family would have to endure extreme ridicule all over again, the challenges of disbelief, and those who didn't believe his story the first time would be making outrageous claims just as they had before. There was always a chance that without the happy ending of last time, they would have ground to accuse the "Spirit-Speaker", as they had called him, of something terrible, something even evil perhaps! What would happen to all his charities and foundations? His good works would be tainted with rumors and lies!

On the other hand…What if this figure wasn't a ghost? If it were human, then people could be in danger. What about Jack?

"Mr. Scrooge?" Bill waited several long seconds, and cleared his throat.

"Mr. Porter," he began shakily. "I have lived a very long life. I have seen things that others have not seen, and I have faced things and come out on the other side of things most people don't even dream about."

Bill nodded, listening intently.

"Right now, I don't know what any of this means, and therefore do not see justification in alarming anyone with the details. The best thing I can do for both of us is to thank you for your hospitality, and to thank God that you felt an irregular urge to tend to your store at such an unusual hour. I took a nasty fall out there, and I couldn't possibly know where to start with the rest of it. But it is over now."

"Mr. Scrooge," Bill answered timidly. "I would be lying if I told you I was not extremely frightened about this."

"I know, I know." Ebenezer nodded warmly, and with good understanding of the position he had placed Bill in. "I need you to trust me. I have many decisions to make, and little time to do it in. I am in no position to go anywhere tonight on foot—"

"Oh, of course not!" Bill interrupted. "You will stay here!"

A moment of silence passed, and Ebenezer took a deep breath, nodding his head. "Yes. I need to rest. I need to think. Tomorrow, early, I will reassess my physical condition, and perhaps then you can send for Dr. Cratchet."

Chapter Twelve

You Came for Me!

"Thank you, Doctor. I'm sure I will be all right."

"Mind you, Mr. Scrooge, I meant what I said. No more walking home alone after dark. You do whatever you need to, making sure to head home early, especially until your knee heals. I think the muscle in your hip will be fine also, just move slowly for a while."

"Yes Bob. I will be fine. Good day."

Bob looked at Ebenezer, weary and worn. He needed rest, but refused to be anywhere besides his office. Bob could not convince the stubborn man to take time off from his responsibilities.

Bob probably suspected that it was because Ebenezer would not allow Tim to come back to work until he had also properly rested and returned well, and with the recent break-in attempt, he would want someone to be there at all times. At this point, he didn't care what anybody suspected or thought. He just wanted to be left alone for a while, and it just so happened that the office was here, and now.

Ebenezer smiled at a quiet Bill standing alone by the door. "Thank you Mr. Porter, for helping me back to the office, and for allowing me to stay at your store last night, but mostly, thank you for helping me in off the street."

"Not at all, Mr. Scrooge."

"Call me Ebenezer."

"Yes sir, Ebenezer sir. You are welcome in my store anytime."

Ebenezer nodded kindly, and turned to Bob.

"Thank you Bob. I will be well enough."

Bill and Bob gathered their things and started toward the door.

"Oh Bob…"

"Yes, Mr. Scrooge?"

"I am going to lay low for a few days. I have some things I need to work out. When your son comes back to work later in the week, I may call upon you to return."

Although Bob didn't completely understand what Mr. Scrooge had in mind, he trusted him.

"Call upon me anytime Mr. Scrooge, medical reasons or otherwise."

"Yes. Thank you both."

The office was quickly quieted.

It was snowing terribly hard outside and the air was bitter cold.

Ebenezer watched through the large window facing the street as children played and threw snowballs at each other. They would appear in small groups, then eventually find interest elsewhere. They giggled and played carelessly.

Ebenezer thought about Jack. He had always seen the child alone, not only without the company of a caretaker, but without the company of another child or friend. He seemed a lonely soul, although his general countenance was youthfully pleasant.

In any case, Ebenezer had a lot to think about.

On the inside, he trembled almost violently every time he thought about the chase the night before. However, he had never allowed his visions or experiences to make him live in fear before, and right now he had more than just himself to think about. Before he could take action, he needed some time alone. He would pray for guidance. Even the slightest wrong move on his part could cause an extreme hysteria, affecting everyone he cared about.

As soon as he had gained enough focus, he closed his eyes and began weighing the pros and cons of every possible action, and prayed about each one.

Soon, hours had gone by since the gentlemen left the office, and Ebenezer sat alone, holding his quill. He had said many prayers, thought many thoughts, and calculated several things. Mostly though, he found that, against his will, he increasingly began to lose clarity in his thinking. It felt as if his brain was slowly narrowing its capacity, and would soon be without thought entirely.

He hadn't really slept in days. He had now been alone for a few hours, and it only felt like a few minutes.

He thought about the possible danger he may be in, and the limitless questions and answers that flew through his mind created a paralyzing wash. His feelings and emotions were many, and each of them contradicted the other and competed for his focus. It had suddenly occurred to him that he was trying to be too many people, and once he acknowledged the thought, he was amazed he had never come to that conclusion before.

He was a best friend, a protector, a fatherly figure, an advisor, a spiritual leader, and a big brother to many, all the while still being seen as a grump, a miser, a spoilsport, a lunatic, and a hermit. So many things that people said about him were true. There was no way out of this never-ending transparent prison where, with any move he made, any move he *didn't* make, he was responsible not only for himself, but for numerous others, a pattern of accountability he could not foresee years ago. For every action he took, there would no doubt be those who supported and those who disagreed with his decision, and now the stakes were high.

The snow had fallen so heavily against the window, he could no longer see beyond the glass. Taking a deep breath, he gently laid his quill on the desk. He turned to face a mirror hanging on the metal hall tree just inside the door. His face looked more aged than it ever had. The lines around his mouth drooped lower than normal. Dark circles hung in bags under his eyes.

"Who are you old man?"

Even he didn't know.

Ebenezer was aware of someone standing outside the office door. The small four-panel window several feet above the knob had darkened and formed into the shape of a person's head about three minutes ago. Whoever it was wasn't knocking or attempting to look in. He simply stood still outside the entrance to the office.

Finally, Ebenezer grabbed his cane and began the struggle to stand. Pain shot through his hip. In a typical day, this would have been the moment that launched several minutes of griping. However, keeping his focus upon the outline of the man outside the door, he winced aloud, and limped forward. No doubt Ebenezer was a little startled, but he was far more stubborn, and refused to let fear get the better of him.

Pursing his lips and shifting his weight on the cane, he reached his hand forward, and cracked the door open.

In only a moment, his eyes adjusted to the light pouring inside, and he squinted, bringing his focus to the short man behind the door.

"Timothy Cratchet!" Ebenezer angrily spouted. "Come inside at once before you catch your death!"

Tim's eyes slowly moved toward Ebenezer.

"Tim! At once! Are you trying to stop an old man's heart?" Ebenezer demanded.

Tim stared, unmoving, save for a few blinks in response to fresh snowflakes on his eyelashes.

Ebenezer felt even more fear welling up inside. Glancing behind Tim, he saw only a few curious townspeople standing at a pause, raising their eyebrows and murmuring about the motionless clerk. Moving his eyes about the surroundings, he saw no immediate threat or signs of injury, yet Tim was not at all well and looked disoriented.

"I beg of you Tim, you're frightening me! Come inside!"

In a sluggish drag, Tim took several lazy steps into the office and said nothing while Ebenezer busied himself to shut and lock the door behind him.

"What has happened?" Ebenezer asked. He continued studying Tim's face, an overwhelming concern causing tears to well up in his eyes.

Tim looked up finally and shook his head. He too, had tears, though they had to have been there a while, as tiny, salt-rivers fell in a thin line down his cheeks, threatening to freeze at the edges.

"Are you alright, my boy?"

Tim turned away, and headed toward his chair, without removing his coat or scarves. Ebenezer hadn't the slightest idea what had happened or what to do now. He simply felt helpless and eager to know what was plaguing Tim. His mind raced with a thousand possible scenarios of what could have been the cause for Tim's abnormal air. Why was Tim even there? He was supposed to be at home with his family, resting from last week's scare with the appearance of the newly feared cloaked figure.

"Did you see it again, Tim?" Ebenezer moved as quickly as his body would allow and stood nervously at his little friend's side.

Tim didn't answer. He sat with a steady flow of tears down his cheeks, despite the lack of heaves or weeping.

Ebenezer shifted in desperation. "I have seen him Tim! I saw him last night! I was going to wait until you arrived here later this week to tell you. Has he threatened you?"

Taking a small breath, and once again lifting his eyes to meet Ebenezer's, Tim finally responded.

"I know who he is and what he wants now."

Ebenezer braced himself at the edge of the desktop, terrified to ask. "You…You do?"

Tim started to shiver. He had been cold for hours, but for some reason, this was the moment his body began to shake.

"Yes I do. He has come for me."

The rawness behind those words being said aloud made Ebenezer's blood drain from his head. Instantly, he started shaking his head in protest. "My boy! What ever do you mean? What in heaven's name would he want with you?" His tears had begun to trickle now too, and his voice trembled as he spoke.

Several long moments passed without a word, and then…

"Ebenezer…" Tim said sadly. "I am dying."

It was as if Ebenezer had swallowed a rock. His stomach wretched and fell solid and still again, as his throat felt like it was closing. His knees threatening to collapse under him, he tightened his grip on the desk and his cane. Tears began flowing like a passionate stream of agony down the old man's wrinkled face.

"No! There's been a mistake! You've been misinformed! What makes you speak such nonsense?"

"When I told you that I was going off to fetch the office supplies…I'm afraid I lied to you. I went to see my father's professor in Liverpool." Tim continued shivering, more and more intensely as the moments went on. "I needed to know the truth."

Ebenezer pounded his cane loudly against the wooden floor in immediate rejection of Tim's news. Helplessness was typically a stranger to him. However if the diagnosis was correct, all of his power, all of his status, and all of his money suddenly seemed so small and insufficient against the reality of poor Tim's fate. If indeed that came about, it would be like losing a son…

"Bah humbug!" He couldn't accept it. "I will see to it that his license is immediately revoked for this! A misdiagnosis of the common cold, nothing more!" Ebenezer moved quickly toward the door, poking his cane about and ranting. "I shall see to it that man never practices medicine again! He's WRONG!" He whipped his head back around to face Tim. "You hear me!? He's absolutely wrong!"

Tim looked up slowly and shook his head.

"No," he said softly, turning his painful stare away from Ebenezer. "No. It makes sense now. The ghost. He is coming for me."

Ebenezer stumbled back a step, caught his tears with the back of his hand, and then cracked his cane against the floor again.

"No! Last night, he was coming for *me*! It does NOT make sense!"

Tim stared straight ahead. He had said all he needed to say, and nothing made any difference now.

He would not speak again.

Ebenezer stood terribly confused, looking at the boy with mixed feelings that a wire whisk itself couldn't have stirred up more effectively. Suddenly, after at least two minutes of painstaking bewilderment, one emotion managed to swell and overcome the rest. There, standing in his office, watching the sweet, helpless young man whose gruesome end had just been foretold, a burst of rage unlike he had ever felt before exploded from within the very depths of his being.

"NO!" he shouted.

Like a madman, he headed for the door and ripped it open, busting the top hinge off from the wood it was mounted to. He hobbled outside, without his jacket, without his scarves, and with nothing on his feet but three layers of hand-knitted socks and some flimsy luxury slippers. With every step, the fury within almost singed the snow from his path. He seemed to be heading in no particular direction, fuming and turning about wildly.

"No! He has a family, you hear me?" After seeing nobody and nothing on the street except the common market shoppers, Ebenezer peered into the sky.

"It's ME you want! Take me, and leave the boy alone!"

People were already gathering a safe distance away in alarm at his explosion. Men clutched their wives and daughters protectively. Even the young teens that had pulled a prank on him the week before were speechless, wide-eyed and mouths agape.

Ebenezer began weeping, staring into the heavens, while snow fell on his hot red face.

"You came for *me* years ago! You came for *me* last night!" His voice cracked. "I will gladly go with you, but LEAVE THE BOY!"

Suddenly a memory invaded his mind, as clear as if it were happening at that exact moment. He heard Jack's voice ringing in his head. "Save him again...save him again..."

"Jack!" Ebenezer shouted. "Jack where are you!?" He brought his attention back to the people around him.

"You there! I need your cart!" Ebenezer hobbled his way through the falling snow and toward the cart. The man who owned the cart also owed Mr. Scrooge money, and out of fearful respect and faith in knowing that if anything happened to his property, Mr. Scrooge was a man who would compensate tenfold, he stepped down quickly, and handed the semi-crippled, shoeless crazy man the reigns. It took a great deal of effort, but after a moment of struggling, Ebenezer's rickety body was in position.

He turned his gaze to the cart-owner and gestured him closer. Ebenezer lowered his voice.

"Dr. Cratchet is at home. Hurry! You must go there and tell the doctor that he is to come at once to Mr. Scrooge's office! Once you have fetched him, go immediately to Liverpool and fetch Dr. Webber. If you need money for a horse or train ticket, tell Dr. Cratchet to give you as much money as you need, and speak of this to no one! Do as I say, and you will be paid handsomely. Hurry! GO NOW!"

The man was stunned and confused, but sensed the urgency in Ebenezer's tone, and after a moment of looking around dumbfounded, he obediently turned to run.

Ebenezer tightened his grip on the reigns.

"I'll find you Jack!"

He nodded at another man nearby, as he spun the cart to leave. The man was a strong, well-mannered, and trustworthy tenant of one of Ebenezer's properties, who was never late with a payment.

"Go to my office, and shut the door! Stay with my clerk and don't let anyone through except Dr. Cratchet or my nephew, Fred! Speak of this to no one else! NO ONE, do you understand? I MUST FIND JACK!"

With that, he turned the cart down the opposing street, and whipped the reigns mercilessly against the horses' backs. Whoever that little Jack boy was, he was the only one with answers, and at any cost, Ebenezer was going to find him.

CHAPTER THIRTEEN

Waiting

Bob held his son's clammy hand, and continued to gently press for answers. "Timothy, where did Mr. Scrooge go? Who is Jack?"

Fred rested his body against the windowsill and shook his head wearily.

Bob gently persisted. "Tim, you've got to answer me, son. We have to find Mr. Scrooge!"

Small vapors of steam danced above three hot mugs of fig pudding, like ghosts against the backdrop of the fire. Thick red wine lay almost untouched. Fred's house was comfortably warm, yet Tim continued to shiver. Bob was still confident in his decision to move Tim to a more safe and secure location than Mr. Scrooge's office, and Fred's house was large enough to comfortably host everyone that mattered the most to Tim.

Tim's eyes were fixed straight ahead at the adjacent bookshelf. His hands were clasped together at his chin while he hunched forward with his elbows on his knees.

Although three men were in the study, the long moments of silence between Bob's gentle prodding, added to what felt like…more than just the absence of sound. It was like the absence of spirit. The sadness and hopelessness in the room was so thick that it seemed to bow the walls.

Bob hadn't felt this measure of despair since his wife had passed away, and now it appeared that he may, in a way, be losing a son.

Timothy didn't look much like his mother, but he had her sweet and optimistic nature. As a boy, even in the hardest of times, everyone who knew him well enough to utter his name knew him to force a smile when everyone else cried. Now that his smile was lost, it looked like everything that made him resemble his mother—everything that made him who he was—was gone. Sitting there, pale, thin, cold, with his bony facial features so concentrated, he resembled a grayish gargoyle like those found in a cemetery.

Bob strengthened his hands around Tim's.

Would now be the moment to tell Timothy the secret? Or would a revelation just make matters worse?

Truth was, at this moment, it didn't seem things could possibly get any worse.

Bob took a deep breath, and started to speak, when Fred interrupted.

"With all do respect Bob, we should let him rest. He wasn't speaking at home. He hasn't spoken for a couple days since Ebenezer left. What makes you think he's going to speak now?"

Bob paused, releasing his fatherly grip, and then closed his eyes, resigned. "Perhaps you are right."

"I will tell Anna and Lillian to turn the beds for the evening."

Bob stood without answering for several seconds. He opened his eyes and looked down at his son. "I suppose rest is the only thing that will benefit anyone at this point."

Nodding, Fred shuffled from his place at the window and started towards the kitchen where the ladies had been worriedly waiting for the past two days.

"Fred—" Bob said suddenly.

"Yes?"

"Thank you so much for allowing my son and his wife and daughter, and, well…me…to stay here while we wait."

Nodding, Fred continued wearily to the next room. Upon entering the kitchen, the two ladies stopped their solemn dialogue and looked up hopefully.

Anna waited with baited breath for a badly needed positive report. When it didn't come, she sat down on a nearby chair and closed her eyes.

"I try to…" Tears welled up against her will. "I try to be positive, but…I fear the worst for little Margaret sometimes. Even without the ability to express herself, it is evident that she senses something is wrong. I fear for Tim as well."

Lillian placed her hand supportively on Anna's shoulder.

"That doesn't make you a bad mother or wife, my dear." She smiled reassuringly. "You just keep praying."

It was sunset, and the snow had stopped collecting for the evening. The cart made a rickety sound as the horses snorted and came to a stop outside of Mr. Scrooge's office. Mr. Scrooge sat silently in the cold for several long minutes before attempting to climb down from his perch on the cart. He was exhausted, and in no mood to deal with putting away horses. He couldn't possibly care less if they all ran away. By all means, he could afford to by all new ones, which was less of a price to pay than to have to mess with them now.

Some noisy shuffling and a minute later, Ebenezer was falling into a comfortable chair just inside the door, awaking Mr. Porter from his nap behind the desk.

"You are here! Finally!"

"Why are you here at all?" Ebenezer answered. "What are you doing in my office, and behind my counter? Where is Tim?"

He instantly started making irritable "shoo" gestures at the unexpected guest while loosening his many layers of clothing.

Mr. Porter completely disregarded Ebenezer's questions and launched into his elation of the old man's return.

"We were all so worried! We didn't know…Where did you…"

"Hush! Have you no sense idiot? Leave me be."

"Yes, Mr. Scrooge. Certainly but—"

"And for heaven's sake, get out of my chair!"

Mr. Porter jumped immediately, straightened his trousers and apron, and headed to tend to the horses outside.

"Mr. Scrooge sir, everyone has been—"

"Go!"

Mr. Porter nodded and closed the door quickly.

Ebenezer had no idea that Mr. Porter was already on his knees outside, earnestly thanking God for the old man's safe return and praying that he would rest through the night. Ebenezer was oblivious to just about everything. His body was numb except for his pounding forehead, and his stomach churned loudly in opposition to the fact that his latest list of priorities did not include stopping for a meal while in pursuit of Jack. He had only slowed down once, grabbed bread from a merchant, and flipped a coin back at him, hastily heading down the street again.

He had looked everywhere for that boy. He had traveled both the main streets and the back streets all over London, calling out his name so many times he had gone hoarse.

Not a moment went by that Jack's young voice didn't echo through his head with those same lingering words. They were vague in the sense that Ebenezer couldn't quote them directly, but he knew that Jack had spoken of saving someone again. Who else but Tim could he possibly be talking about, and if it *was* Tim, why would Jack know anything about it, and furthermore, why was Jack always around at a bad time, but nowhere to be found when he was needed?

Over and over again throughout the last few days, he tried to assemble puzzle pieces together and ended up coming short. He knew so little about Jack. Even the details about his parents were obscure at best.

Through the streets he had traveled, he saw many boys that fit Jack's profile, but none that answered to the name Jack, and many that turned their heads and looked very different from front view. Every time he saw a well-dressed boy, he would call out to them, and often received concerned expressions from the parents if they were accompanied. Once or twice, a child had even answered as if that were his name, and appeared extremely confused when Ebenezer would examine his face, and then throw his hands up in frustration and whip the horses harder.

One small girl who looked very boyish was attempting to break in to a bakery late the night before, and ran away quickly when she realized she had been seen. Ebenezer had followed her for thirteen streets before realizing that it was a little homeless girl. On any other occasion, he would have warmly invited her on to his cart, and drove her to a hot meal…

His stomach rumbled again.

Turning to the cupboard next to the safe, he noticed some small soup crackers on the middle shelf next to an ornate glass salt shaker. He often took his meals while continuing to focus on his money counting. Up until the last week, when everything went awry, very little thrilled him more than counting money, and now his previous unwillingness to leave his favorite hobby, even for a meal, proved to be a blessing.

Glancing about the room, he noticed a high cupboard above Tim's desk that to his memory might have contained half a loaf of bread from Tim's lunch several days earlier. Under the circumstances, he was sure Tim wouldn't mind if he ate it.

When he pulled the cupboard door open, office supplies flooded out onto the floor, hitting Ebenezer on the way down. There were inkwells galore, a very large roll of parchment that would be sure to leave a knot on his head, and numerous feather quills with no trace of ink on them anywhere. Apparently this was where Tim had hidden the supplies the previous week to secure his trip to Liverpool.

Instantly enraged by the thud on the head caused by improperly stored parchment, Ebenezer pulled a quill that had somehow drifted down and attached itself to his scarf, and tore it to shreds in anger, throwing the white feather pieces all over the room. On his way back to his chair with the few crackers he had found, a fallen inkwell suffered a hard, angry kick, thrusting it against the wall.

Soon he had devoured the crackers, stopping only here and there to mutter about poorly hidden supplies, and found himself thankful for the fire Mr. Porter had kept going while he was gone. It had been several long days since he had felt warmth on his skin. He didn't want to stop to sleep, but knew he didn't have the strength to fight it any longer.

He had left his office without shoes. While on the cart, he noticed a riding blanket, which he wrapped his feet in. Now however, after having walked through the snow to his office, his slippers, along with his outermost pair of three socks were wet. Quickly, he removed them to keep the others as dry as possible.

It hadn't been a restful trip, but at least he wasn't on foot, and as stiff as he felt now, it was good to have the weight off his hip and knee.

Leaning back, he pulled his coat tight around his body, and took in a deep breath, resigned to the temptation of slumber, if only for a short time. Then he planned to set out to find the others. He wasn't looking forward to being asked a trillion questions of his whereabouts and made to account for this "Jack" person, whose name he had screamed just before he rode away in the cart. But he was desperate to know how Tim was doing and anxious to check in on the rest of his family. Then he would have a sit-down with Bob, explaining all he knew about the cloaked ghost and Dr. Webber, that was of course if Tim hadn't already told everyone...The list of responsibility ahead of him was far too long for him to take on here and now, without at least a few minutes of rest.

Chapter Fourteen

Drifting Off to Death

Moments into Ebenezer's sleep, he began dreaming that he was a boy again, walking through an elaborate orchard. His sister was singing a sweet nursery melody somewhere very close. He tried to follow her voice, but it sounded like it was drifting consistently away from him. The area was wide open where he stood amidst lavish apple trees and plump grapevines.

He listened…

"Little ladies dancing, in blue satin shoes, singing songs of roses, as they receive the cues…"

The air was so sweet, like the smell of a hundred different exotic flowers mingling with fresh, supple fruit, and the only other sound besides his sister's song was the occasional thud of over-ripened apples hitting the ground. The sun cast warm rays of sunlight on beautiful plants that then reflected their spectacular colors in all directions. The very grass beneath his feet seemed to glow…

Of course! It was Mr. Fezziwig's property! And what a beautiful property it was. Ebby used to love the days when his father would gather the family for a social call and head to Mr. Fezziwig's place so he could pretend to fit in with the elitist rich folk.

Mr. Fezziwig was a tall, boisterous man, built like Father Christmas, and he too, had a merry laugh that rang from his lungs and penetrated walls, floors, or whatever else was around. He used to grip his enormous hands around Ebby's biceps, which at the time couldn't compete with the size of a poor man's sausage link, and say, "One of these days lad, you'll be workin' fer me! Just keep that smile on m'boy, and you'll be me warehouse manager!" Then he would slap him on the back and invite him to join the adults in whatever game they were playing.

Ebenezer would always remember the effect old Fezziwig had on people. No child felt treated like a child. No poor man was treated lower class. No woman's opinion was shoved aside in the presence of men. He was loved and trusted by everyone, especially little Ebenezer.

"Ebby!"

There she was, between an apple tree and a cherry tree, in a dark purple dress, her blond hair in long ringlets.

"What are you doing, silly?"

Ebenezer smiled at his sister. "I was looking for you. I heard you singing, and Father sent me out to find you. I was going to jump out and scare you."

She giggled at having already outwitted his scheme, and ran to meet him in the opening between the trees. Ebenezer took his sister's hand and they walked together in the direction of the grand, ivory-colored house.

"I'm so glad that Father sent for you to come home for the summer this year instead of sending you away to that lousy boarding school."

Ebenezer's smile faded. "I doubt that is the way that he wanted it."

"Oh Ebby, I don't care! You're here now, and I missed you so!"

Ebenezer scowled. "Well, I can't say I missed *him* any."

She wasn't about to correct him. The way their father treated him was often cold and unfair, and she knew it. His school reports could slip to just under perfect, and he was scolded and lectured for hours. When he did reach academic perfection, it was only enough to earn a stern expression, as if he was being warned to stay at that standard. Not a day went by that their father didn't remind Ebenezer about the importance of success, the importance of balanced finances, and the importance of providing for his own spoiled children someday. It was no wonder that in some ways the summer boarding school was far less exhausting than his trips home during vacations.

It wasn't just that he was hard on him. There was a complete lack of any father-son relationship whatsoever.

"Father tries, you know. He means well."

"Yes, I know. I know he does. I just wish he'd…"

Ebenezer chose for his sister's sake not to finish his statement.

A moment passed between them and she glanced ahead toward the house.

"I'll race you!"

Ebenezer's smile returned, and he burst into a run. He kept his sights on the house for a few moments, and by the time he glanced back, she was gone.

Completely vanished within the blink of an eye.

The garden had disappeared, and everything was black.

"Hello?"

No answer. Just blackness as far as the eye could see.

"Where are you?"

Still nothing.

Ebenezer started to spin around, frantically looking for anything or anybody, and with much concern for his sister.

Slowly, the light returned.

He was now eighteen, and in Mr. Fezziwig's ballroom. As the surroundings became clearer, Ebenezer turned about, noting the sudden change.

Giant, elaborate cherubs in gold stood proudly in the center of the open space. Piano music was filtering in through the windows from the next room. High gloss embellished the hard wood flooring under the massive chandeliers and candelabras. On the farthest wall was a large fireplace with several paintings of Mr. and Mrs. Fezziwig, sitting with their daughter, Belle, at several different ages.

She had been beautiful since the beginning.

Distracted by Belle's portrait for the moment, Ebenezer forgot everything else that had happened. He started toward the picture, a smile developing on his handsome young face.

Something twitched in his peripheral vision.

He looked to the right, and saw nothing, though he was sure something had scurried past. The only movement now was the flickering of the candles in a slight breeze by the window.

Hoping to convince himself that was all it was, he continued toward the paintings, walking slow and alert as he glanced about.

A strange, unearthly giggle came from somewhere in the room, giving Ebenezer chills. Holding his breath, a knot formed in his gut. Within seconds, his forehead had begun to collect beads of sweat.

He looked left and right, unable to see anything out of the ordinary, though the presence of something intensely evil was suddenly suffocating him from all directions.

Finally, Ebenezer *did* see something. There was a large brown door at the far right of the room, which lead to a closet that was typically used for wine storage. The door was closed seconds ago. Now, the door was slightly cracked, and two very penetrating, wide-open eyes could be seen quite clearly from inside.

Not knowing what inspired him, Ebenezer bolted forward, running toward the door. The eyes quickly vanished in an array of evil cackling, as Ebenezer's hand thrust the entrance open.

Inside the light was dim, and he could see Mr. Fezziwig himself slumped in a corner, head down, and unmoving. His skin was ashen gray, and blood was trickling from somewhere on his body and onto the floor.

Other than that horrific sight, the room was wall to wall empty.

"M...Mr. Fezziwig, sir?"

There was no answer.

He was frightened.

"Mr. Fezziwig? Wake UP! Are...Are you...?"

Ebenezer rushed to the collapsed body. He gripped his thin fingers around Fezziwig's plump arm, and as he pulled, Fezziwig's eyes moved slowly up to face him.

Where his eyes should have been, there were black, fleshy, swollen bulbs, strangely void of life, yet very alert and aware of his presence.

They blinked.

Ebenezer froze in fear.

Saying nothing, he managed to stagger away several steps. Fezziwig didn't move other than to blink while he stared, and let his mouth hang open lethargically.

Then, his sister's voice could be heard once again singing her melody, yet this time, it sounded hauntingly sing-song and unnatural.

"Little ladies dancing, in blue satin shoes..."

Ebenezer spun around to face the ballroom, and saw nothing unusual. Miscellaneous books, wineglasses, dance cards, and feathered fans were strung about as if an entire party of people had left their things behind, but nothing frightening appeared to be present.

"Where are you?" he questioned the air.

He had hoped for an answer from his darling younger sister.

"Singing songs of death, as the spirits pay their dues..."

Her innocent voice deliberately twisting the words sent creepy goose pimples down his arms and legs.

Turning back, Mr. Fezziwig's black pits were still fixed on Ebenezer, and the body hadn't moved an inch.

A small but strong hand took his wrist so forcefully from behind, that its thin fingers tore into the tender muscle tissue in Ebenezer's hand. Gasping in pain, he spun to face his little sister, now hovering three feet above the floor. Her eyes met his, though her chin was almost completely touching her shoulder at a contorted ninety degree angle.

"Are you afraid Ebby?" she taunted, eyes wide.

"Yes," he said honestly. "I'm terrified."

She grotesquely stretched her mouth open until her jaw was literally waist length, and loud screaming from all directions erupted in his ears. Her face drained from its natural color, and her flesh dropped off into disintegrating pools on the floor.

"Are you scared of your little sister, old man?" Her voice was now made up of several voices, at different pitches.

Wildly cackling, she tightened her grip so supernaturally tight that it severed Ebenezer's left hand completely.

Screaming in agony, he fell to the floor and closed his eyes tight.

"What is all this? What is happening!?"

Continuous laughing and screeching from all around invaded Ebenezer's head. He was writhing in misery on the floor, his own wailing in near harmony with the unholy weeping now surrounding him.

It was like ten thousand entities were closing in on him.

Choking...he was choking...

No room to breathe…

Opening his eyes, he was now surrounded by the evil doppelgangers of many whom in life he loved and trusted. One by one they appeared, every one more frightening and evil than the last.

Beginning with Mr. Fezziwig, they all grew closer to him, their terrifying intentions written all over their grotesque, disfigured faces.

Ebenezer knew in his gut that it was over for him if he didn't find a way out. Turning onto his stomach, still struggling to breathe, he crawled with one arm away from them, but the moment that he began to make a few inches progress, great explosions of fire shot up from the floor, merging together to form a wall. The flames were so close to his face, they scorched his nostrils and singed his eyebrows.

Looking back, the terrifyingly familiar things from the underworld were upon him. The one that looked like his sister already had her strong hands on his ankles.

Evil behind him…

Fire in front…

Nowhere to run…

Now he was unable to breathe at all.

Ebenezer felt his strength fading. His lungs felt fully collapsed, and his body tingled like needles all over. He could feel sharp fingernails digging their way up his back, and the fire was now blistering his face.

He was officially cornered, and couldn't fight.

The room started to go black.

He felt his eyes close slowly.

From the chaos of the deafening sounds of screaming, wailing, and corrupted cackling, one powerful, yet gentle voice spoke out very clearly, uttering only one word.

"Awaken."

Opening his eyes, Ebenezer found his face positioned only inches from the bottom of the fire screen on his office floor. His face felt like it was on fire, and his scarf was wound around his neck so tightly that it had nearly cut off his airway. Attempting to remove his scarf, he quickly realized he only had use of one hand. Using every ounce of his strength, he kicked himself onto his back, paying no attention to the cracking sounds his stiff bones made, and with his right hand, pulled the scarf forcefully away from his neck. Gasping for air, he lifted his arm and saw that his left hand was thankfully still intact. It seemed he had fallen asleep with his weight on his wrist while his hand was bent backward. It would be a while before the pain in his wrist was gone and his fingers would have full feeling in them again.

"These dreams…"

Ebenezer remembered his little sister's face…

"They will be the death of me."

Fred tried not to be irritated by the sound of frantic rapping on the door first thing in the morning, only hours after his household had finally begun to get some rest. It might have been an update on his uncle, and he would never forgive himself if he missed his return.

Anna was one step ahead of him, carrying the baby toward the front door. He wasn't entirely sure how long he had been sleeping through the noise. Rising from his makeshift bed on the couch since his own bed was occupied by his guests, he followed her curiously.

The bright sun against the snow outside cast a blinding light into the entryway of the house, causing Anna and Fred to shield their eyes. Regardless however of their inability to focus on their visitor, his voice revealed his identity immediately.

"Fred, Anna, I come with news."

Mr. Porter's voice was very reserved. Fred instantly rushed to pull the door wide open.

"Good news? Or…"

Mr. Porter hesitated for a moment before giving his answer.

"I…believe you will find it good and bad news."

Anna backed into the house far enough that she could stop squinting and study his face.

"Is it *very* bad news that accompanies your good news, friend?" she finally brought herself to ask.

His silence was enough of an answer. Fred found himself losing patience quickly. His typical easygoing nature could not apply when it came to bad news of his uncle.

"Mr. Porter, I beseech you! Have it out at once! What is this news you bring?"

Nodding, Mr. Porter brushed past them and began speaking immediately.

"Mr. Scrooge has returned."

Fred closed the door behind them quickly, while Anna whispered an eager, "Oh thank God."

"He arrived at the office around dusk last night, and demanded to be left alone."

"You left him alone?"

"Yes." Mr. Porter began nervously pacing. "I would have come straight here, but I had a feeling I should stay close to him and at least make sure that he was safe through the night. You must understand how I would feel responsible if I had abandoned him only to find out later that whoever or *what*ever this Mr. Jack individual is he's involved with right now had endangered him in any way."

They nodded. Anna cupped a hand over her mouth in a nervous motion, swallowed the stubborn lump that had collected in the back of her throat, and then snuggled little Margaret closer to her bosom. Fred took a deep breath, determined to remain calm.

"I took the cart and horses to my own personal stables and then spoke with my wife. I told her to go to Mr. Scrooge's house and let our son know that he could stop keeping watch there at his personal residence. By the time I had readied the cart again to come here and tell you of his arrival, I walked to the street just opposite his office to check on him again, and there was a shadow cast on the back of his curtains, as if he was moving about."

At this, Mr. Porter cleared his throat, and closed his eyes momentarily steadying his emotions.

"I wanted to make positive that he was alright, so I let myself in. He is refusing to see anyone but Dr. Cratchet."

"Is he alright!?" Fred exploded.

Mr. Porter cleared his throat and again forced back emotions.

"He made me promise not to talk to anyone about it until after he has seen the doctor."

"Where is he now, good friend?" Anna interjected.

"He is here. Outside."

"Is he…Is he…Is…" Fred fumbled for words, stood speechless and overwhelmed for a few moments, and then turned quickly on his heel and sprinted for the back of the house. He was entirely unconcerned with anything but the safety of his uncle, which led him to barging in completely on his guest.

"BOB! Wake up immediately! You must come quick!"

Bob awoke in a startled jolt and took a second to realize it was not a dream. He blinked, remembered where he was, and then sprung forward in his bed and focused his eyes on his terrified host. Completely dazed, he squinted his stare on the doorway of the room. He trusted Fred, and knew his tone of urgency was justification enough to follow him immediately with no explanation necessary.

Throwing his blankets aside, and leaping into his slippers, he followed Fred through the long hallway, stumbling once, but recovering well. Fred offered a panic-stricken explanation on the way.

"My uncle is back, but something is wrong, and he will see no one but you!"

Bob saw Mr. Porter standing nervously with his hand on the knob of the front door, and nodded instinctively.

Blinded by the initial shock of the sunlight reflecting off billions of settled snowflakes, he threw his arms up and ran while keeping his eyes on Mr. Porter's footsteps in the snow. Snow lodged its way deeply into the doctor's slippers as he ran, which was the least of his worries.

Finally approaching the cart he lowered his arm and allowed his eyes to come into focus…

"Oh merciful heavens," Bob said sadly. He spent only a moment studying what he saw before switching into his detached, medical emergency demeanor.

"Bill, my good man," Bob began in the usual calm, mechanical tone he used when it meant bad news. "Get me my supplies, in a black briefcase under the guest bed." He turned and faced Mr. Porter.

"Tell Lillian to fetch some snow from the *back* of the property, as we don't want anybody coming out this way, and pack it into some sterile cloths. Instruct Fred to start a very mild fire in the study, and pour some wine for the pain. Have Anna keep the children in the back bedrooms until we find a tactful way to prepare them for this."

Bob hesitated a moment longer, and with a heavy sigh and a sorrowfully convinced nod, he turned to face Ebenezer in the cart again.

"He is terribly, terribly burned."

Mr. Porter had seen the reaction he was afraid of, and from the doctor himself. He nodded, and ran toward the house, stifling his tears for a later hour.

CHAPTER FIFTEEN

Cloaked Indeed

Try not to move that eye, Mr. Scrooge. You will need to keep it shut and covered for several days. Luckily it is just the outer skin area that suffered any damage, but you must still keep it closed."

"And just how do you expect me to see to my duties with one measly eye, when I can't even see well with the both of them anymore?"

"Mr. Scrooge, try not to speak. You are aggravating the corner of your mouth again."

Bob continued to apply the salve to the burns on his neck and made sure to speak in calm, gentle tones. Ebenezer winced loudly at almost every move Bob made.

"And besides, you're lucky you have both eyes left. This volume of heat exposure should have blinded you completely."

"Don't you 'lucky' me Bob Cratchet! Look at my face! All I needed is one more reason to invite people to stare, and now I'm a bloody monster!" He yelled as loud as he could, with only the use of half of his mouth. His face hurt tremendously.

"You're lucky to be alive is what you are."

"I should start charging a shilling per person to enter the office!

We could go into business together you and I—'Step right up folks, come see the only half-man half-beast in London!'"

"Your lip, Mr. Scrooge."

Ebenezer scoffed angrily. "Well I don't appreciate—"

"Close your mouth please."

"Humbug…"

"Shhhh."

"Ouch!"

Bob was an incredibly good doctor, who took pride not only in his work, but fulfillment in making people well and improving family's lives. Everyone knew he had been through enough with his own family that he would understand taking a personal interest in every diagnosis, and he charged a fraction of most medical professionals in the area. Often he would make visits for free when a family could not afford the bill…It was all too fresh in his memory of the days when he could not afford Tiny Tim's expenses. He would forever be in debt to Mr. Scrooge for his intervention on that part.

Bob turned his eyes once again to the kitchen's entrance to ensure Mr. Scrooge's privacy. He walked to the basin to rinse his hands using one of the cloths that Lillian had laid out.

"I regret to inform you that this will feel a bit restrictive for a while. I believe that you will get used to it though."

Bob dried his hands and retrieved the gauze from his black case. Slowly, he wrapped it around Ebenezer's neck and chin, and then up to his forehead, taking special care not to move any of the delicate flesh hanging off the burns for now. Bob cringed with sympathy as he looked at the now quiet, shrunken man with melted and blistered skin, knowing that in the next couple weeks, most of what was left of his face would die and fall off, leaving an extremely disfigured map of what he was. He felt terribly sorry for all Ebenezer had been through, but the hard, cold truth of it was that right now Ebenezer was in shock and couldn't begin to fathom what was yet to come. Almost his entire body was throbbing, but numbly from the whole experience, and soon the most agonizing physical pain of his life would ensue. He would go through massive loss of facial tissue, with probable infection, followed by a long and gruesome healing process. Bob could see in advance that Ebenezer could very possibly cause more complications because of his impatience and lack of cooperation.

"There you are. That will do for now. Are you in a great deal of pain?"

"What do *you* think?" Ebenezer mumbled.

"I will have to remove these wrappings in a few hours so they don't adhere to the wound, and the salve will help prevent the surface burns from reaching any deeper, which will also help take out some sting later on. The good news is that I was able to remove the pieces of scarf that were lodged in your neck without much difficulty."

Ebenezer couldn't nod without pain, and talking caused the corner of his mouth to rip. He simply sat, acknowledging the words silently. He would save his lips for the talk they were about to have with Tim, Fred, Anna, and Lillian.

"I will speak with Lillian and devise a soft-food diet for you, but I want you to keep sipping the wine, I know you don't like drinking wine from a teaspoon, however I think it will help maintain a manageable pain level for now."

Again, Ebenezer said nothing.

Bob took a seat, facing Ebenezer directly, and gave a soft smile.

Ebenezer stared back with his right eye, and sighed.

"Mr. Scrooge…as your friend, I want to say so many things…"

They both sat for several seconds looking at each other, a grave truth in Bob's eyes caused a nervous twitch in the pit of the old man's stomach. Ebenezer knew exactly what was coming.

"And as a doctor?" he prompted from the side of his mouth.

"As…As a doctor, Mr. Scrooge, I must tell you…" Bob cleared

his throat and closed his eyes. One solitary moment passed, and he quickly corrected his bad decision to sit down with his friend face to face. Soon he was behind him once more, loading his instruments back into his case.

Suddenly for the first time, Dr. Cratchet did not want to be a doctor.

"Ahem...As a doctor, I must tell you that you will never look the same again. You feel much less pain right now than you will in the coming days, and I will require your full cooperation to accelerate your healing. Some of the things that I will have to do, you are not going to like. However, fighting against me will not be an option if you want to take the least painful road to recovery."

Ebenezer remained silent.

In all of Bob's years as his clerk, he longed for a day when he could speak matter-of-factly to his boss without hearing cross threats or heavy complaining. But in their years as friends, Bob grew to find Ebenezer's quick and snappish remarks endearing. At this moment, he would give anything to hear Mr. Scrooge's typical grouchy quips and sneers. However there and then, his friend's silence hit him like a barrel of rocks. He squeezed his eyes shut, cleared his throat and quickly left the room, leaving his instruments behind him.

Making his way into the living room where everyone was waiting with baited breath for an update, Bob let out a few sobs, and then quickly regained his composure.

"I'm sorry." He cleared his throat loudly and ran his fingers through his hair. "Fred, you may see him now, but you can't say anything that upsets him, and please keep your conversation to questions he can answer with a yes or no."

Fred stood, and just before leaving the room, Bob gripped his arm and lead him into the hallway.

"He almost choked to death. That's why the fire didn't wake him."

"What fire?" Fred asked suddenly.

"He had probably already been unconscious and fading out for several minutes without air before he struggled toward the fireplace in his office. From what I gather, he was dreaming that he had just lain down to die. I'm fairly sure that his dream was but seconds away from becoming a reality."

Bob knew that none of his words were easy to hear or understand at this point.

Fred looked horrified.

"Your uncle literally escaped death last night."

Fred looked down at the floor, completely speechless.

"I'm sorry, there is no way to prepare you for what you are about to see."

Bob quickly moved the conversation on. Not only were there so many details that needed arranging, but the longer Fred lingered in the hallway, the harder it would be to face his uncle. These moments were rushed, just as Bob felt they needed to be.

"I am going to get Tim up and out of bed. I'm going to explain to him what is going on, because I think he has a right to know. Perhaps with the four of us all together, we can…work this whole thing out."

Fred nodded with respect, swallowed hard, and continued toward the kitchen.

Upon entering, he covered his mouth in shock, and stumbled sideways into a dinette chair.

"Oh Uncle…"

"I'm sorry Nephew. Do I frighten you?"

"No no no no." Fred started to cry. "You don't frighten me, Uncle. I'm…I'm so terribly sorry! How did…How can I…I'm…"

Once again speechless, Fred just shook his head, and allowed a few tears to trickle down his cheeks.

The sight of his uncle so damaged was heartbreaking. His dearest relative outside his immediate family was somehow spared death, which was something to rejoice about. Yet the sight of him this way made rejoicing an impossibility.

"Now you know why I wouldn't see any of you until I had spent time with Bob."

Fred nodded and wiped away several tears.

As Fred was finally gearing himself up to speak, Bob suddenly rushed in and interrupted.

"Timothy's missing!"

Ebenezer only needed one millisecond to process this information, and then stood up immediately, disregarding any pain from sudden movement. "No! We have to find him NOW!" he shouted.

Bob shook his head and began gesturing for him to sit back down.

Seeing Bob's immediate reserve, Ebenezer realized he would have to be a force the others could not reckon with. He pounded his fist on the table hard, and yelled and growled loudly, splitting the corner of his mouth open. A stunned nephew and friend stood silent, waiting to hear an explanation, which Ebenezer gave at once.

"You don't understand! We don't have TIME! You don't know what is going on with him, and I DO! Do NOT argue with me, either of you! I will NOT be stopped!" He tried to shake away an image of the blade-bearing, cloaked figure as it shoved its way into his head.

Bob felt suddenly terrified by the reality and the danger of the situation. "Mr. Scrooge, calm yourself! What is going on!?"

Ebenezer walked several steps toward Bob, put his hand on his shoulder and squeezed. Having his full attention, he lowered his stare. "I will tell you everything, as soon as we find your son. That is a promise I will not break."

"Is he in danger?"

"Yes. Most certainly."

Bob's face went white, and he felt his toes go numb.

Fred reached out and grabbed Ebenezer by the arm.

"Uncle, we will go. You must stay here."

An enormous, angry snarl immediately burst forth from Ebenezer, as he responded to his nephew's concern with a great shove. Fred was caught off guard, and plunged backward into a heavy wooden butcher-block table.

Looking up, he saw years of accumulated sorrow and regret in the old man's eyes. A fuming intensity showed through his injuries, and even the layers of gauze. His teeth were bared, jaw clenched, and nostrils, just visible under his wraps, were flared wide in an expression of absolute resolution.

Fred didn't have time to take this reaction personally. He was terribly scared for his uncle and fumbled for a moment to steady himself for another protest. Before he had time to say a word, Ebenezer spoke.

"I love you Fred," he said fiercely, not noticing the bit of spittle that shot out as he spoke. "But I pity the man that stands in my way of looking for Tim. If it were either of you in danger out there, I would do the same."

Bob reached his arm out in attempt to calm him.

"Don't touch me Bob Cratchet! So help me I won't hold back! I'm warning you!" He spat, lifting his cane to the air threateningly.

"Mr. Scrooge, you could DIE out there!"

"Your son WILL die out there!"

The three of them were silent for a moment. Bob and Fred exchanged glances with each other, and back again. Ebenezer looked like a complete lunatic, holding his cane high above their heads.

A part of Bob was flattered by Ebenezer's unmitigated determination in finding his son. The doctor side of him saw complete disaster.

"Listen to me, both of you," Ebenezer said pleadingly, tightening his grip on the cane even more. "I must save him…Again."

"Again?" Bob shook his head, still confused.

"THERE IS NO TIME TO EXPLAIN!" Ebenezer shouted.

Facing his mummified friend, whose reasoning he had no choice but to accept, he nodded, swallowed, and looked at Fred.

"It is his own death Mr. Scrooge chooses." He looked at Ebenezer again, blatant pity written across his pleasant features.

"If I am going to die…" he painfully blinked his swollen eyelids.

His own voice resonated the memory of sixteen years earlier when he had last spoken these heartless words to the portly gentlemen asking for donations to give to orphans and poverty-stricken folk who would choose death over going to a prison or workhouse.

"Then they had better do it and decrease the surplus population."

His rebuke had been merciless.

The irony of his own life seemed of such inconsequence when one so precious to him was at stake. He felt the pangs of his old heart's judgment against himself.

Ebenezer was determined. "If I am to die, then I'd better well do it and decrease the surplus population."

Fred remembered the story well, and recognized his uncle's words. He gulped, took a long, hard look at Ebenezer, and wearily shook his head. "Let's split up."

Ebenezer brought his arm back to himself, and pulled his coat over his wound, pulling several layers of gauze and salve out of place. Turning his wrist in small circles and grumbling in pain, he hobbled for the front door, passing two small, frightened children, Anna, Mr. Porter, and Lillian.

Bob was right behind him, shouting out orders for Lillian to follow the men, and for Anna to stay with the children.

. . .

Fred and Lillian headed to the market district. Bob went first to check the office, with plans to go to Tim and Anna's house after that. Mr. Porter would continue to run the cart, keeping an eye out on every street. Ebenezer headed toward the train station.

As he walked, people stopped dead in their tracks to stare, point, whisper, and judge as never before. Ebenezer hardly noticed them as he plowed through them, weaving between them, moving as fast as he could. As he turned his head about, he felt small fragments of skin tearing throughout his face and neck, and each movement was like a thousand needles fresh from a bonfire being nailed into every square inch of his face. Somehow though, up against Tim's safety, he would force himself to believe that it seemed no more difficult to endure than a slight skin rash.

He would find him.

"Spirits…Don't you dare…"

He *would* find him…

Through crowd after crowd, he limped quickly, struggling through the falling snow, severe burns causing each moment to seem like an eternity of hellfire.

Eventually, he rounded the last corner before the train station, and into the mass of people loading and unloading their things for Christmas travel. Once again paying no attention to the stares and occasional frightened screams, he headed directly to the ticket booth, only vaguely noticing someone quietly saying, "Look out for the monster," and gripping a small girl by the arm as he passed.

"Timothy Cratchet come this way? A young, thin man by the name of Timothy Cratchet?"

The man behind the counter never even turned his gaze to the window. He simply continued to unenthusiastically stamp the incoming arrivals and shuffle papers.

"Not that I know of this mornin'. Took a train to Liverpool last week, but I think he only had a two-day pass, and he woulda been back by now."

"Thank you, sir." Ebenezer turned quickly. This was one moment that he was glad Tim had to travel so far for the special supplies. It ended up a fortunate coincidence that the man behind the booth recognized his name.

From one conductor to another, Ebenezer made progress around the main boarding area of the station where passengers from London were most likely to be.

Either they were afraid to answer honestly because of his appearance, or they had in fact not seen a young man who fit Timothy's description anywhere this morning. Either way, he decided it was best to keep moving.

He headed immediately to the passengers in the ticket line and walked the opposite direction they were facing, scanning their faces. After shocking several people and putting one woman into complete hysterics, he concluded that Tim was not leaving on any of the next several trains at least.

He wasn't entirely sure where to look next as he headed for the exit out of the station, but he kept moving quickly. It was difficult to breathe and move around with gauze covering his skin.

A large arrival of passengers from a neighboring town flooded into the entryway, hugging relatives, shedding tears of reunion, carrying luggage, and completely blocking Ebenezer's path.

"Excuse me mister! Get out of the way you idiot!"

Over and over attempting to throw his voice above the masses, he pushed onward, oblivious to people's reactions to him, and finally met an opening outside the train station.

Just at the edge of the crowd, something caught Ebenezer's eye.

How could *that* be?

A very pretty woman stood not far away, looking down the street leading to the marketplace. She appeared to be about the age of forty-five, and was travelling alone. Her beautiful blond curls were collecting snow as she paused at the curb to kick loose the compacted fluff from her boot heels.

Attempting to get a better look at her face, two elderly ladies stepped right in his line of vision. Quickly shifting around them, and pushing a heavyset man into his wife, Ebenezer caught sight of her again, this time walking very slowly toward the busiest of London's shopping districts.

There were far too many people in the way for him to follow her without fear of her taking a sudden change in direction and disappearing. Part of his fear was based on the abundance of small alleyways that he now suspected she had substantial knowledge of...He would have to catch up, but stealthily, so as not to direct too much attention upon himself.

Turning left, he slid down an alleyway and stumbled to the other side. Another alleyway straight ahead, moving fast, and then one to the right, and he was directly behind her. From here, he could hobble closely behind without having to mingle with a crowd.

She moved very slowly and casually, taking in the surroundings. She stopped only once more, standing under a lonely awning, to roll down her sleeves and cover her pretty hair, all the while pretending to be casual.

Pretending to be innocent...

He wasn't sure before, but the dark purple cloak was unmistakable now that she was fully draped in it. Ebenezer had only ever seen one like it, with its long velvety waves of fabric flowing to the ground and a large slack-filled hood that draped lazily about the shoulders, yet just stiff enough at the forehead that it could almost blacken the face even in daylight.

The race had begun.

Scrambling once again through crowds and weather, Ebenezer moved quickly to reach her.

Though it seemed she was still oblivious to his pursuit, she moved at a dramatically agile speed, just as she had done that night. It was as if she didn't have to try. Long legs carried her from one alleyway to another, no doubt at just a fraction of her potential speed, and yet she moved silently, and without notice from anyone else. Her movements rippled her thin cloak in the same unique way that he'd seen before.

Finally she slowed down, only a half mile from his office. Not moving an inch, she stood almost perfectly still for about a minute, which allowed Ebenezer to catch up and move rather close.

She appeared to be watching the patrons on the street, and as silent as the grave, she hovered against the wall. There were just enough people walking around that Ebenezer's steps blended in with the commotion.

One more step…

Two more steps…

At last, he was just close enough to jab her with his cane if he would have wanted. More intelligently though, he brought his cane high into the air, and down hard on the bottom of her cloak. Feeling the tug, she turned instantly to face him.

"The hood! Off with it!"

CHAPTER SIXTEEN

Melody

Tim walked the last few steps to his hiding place of choice. Stepping over the edge of the marble wall carefully, he then flattened his back against it, slid down, and just stared.

He had never noticed the ceiling in this place before. How brilliantly elaborate it was! Made from wood of the finest selection, it was laid carefully board by board, and artfully hand carved. The natural shades alternated from light to dark, darkest at the edges, and lightest in the middle at the arch, with colossal rafters supporting the hanging candelabras every ten feet or so.

This was his favorite place in the world.

Of course they would think to look for him in this room, but they wouldn't think to look behind the marble wall.

He sighed heavily and tried to pretend he wasn't colder than he had ever been in his life. If he tried, he could literally feel the life slipping out of him moment to moment.

His eyes drifted from the ceiling to the great sculpture in front of him. This was yet another thing he had never appreciated so closely. It was very artistic how the entire piece of art was a standard ivory color, except at the head, hands, and feet, where the thorns and nails were. The artist had specifically painted in the blood in those areas…

For a moment, Tim felt convicted.

He couldn't imagine the suffering that *He* must have gone through...

It made Tim's own physical infirmity seem a little less significant.

He thought for a moment, and then brushed away the nagging sensation as easily as it came.

It didn't matter anyway...

He was here now, and he didn't want to be bothered.

Moments passed, as they stared at each other. Ebenezer was somewhat impressed by her lack of fear. Unlike most he had encountered that day, she didn't even flinch at the sight of him and his terribly injured skin. Instead, she simply regained her tall stance and squared her shoulders. For a few long moments, she just stared back from the shadows of her hood, and then, slowly pulled it back.

He was struck with bewilderment when he saw her up close for the first time. His fingers and toes went numb, and his cheeks began to ignite, sending a throb to his already burning face. His heart began to pound in his ears.

How could this be?

Gripping the dark cloth in her hands, she jerked it out from under his cane proudly, and then calmly folded her arms at her front. She tilted her head up, and focused her electric blue eyes on him. At her full height, she was at least six inches taller than he.

Oh how she resembled her!

Ebenezer dropped his cane, and spread the medical wrapping

away from his left eye, so he could make sure he was making proper use of all his senses. He couldn't believe what he saw!

The woman drew in a heavy sigh and cocked her head to the side condescendingly.

"Well…Ebenezer…Grand, wonderful Ebenezer…So good to finally meet you. You look terrible."

Far more interested in who she was than her childish banter, he simply shook his head.

"You look like someone I…What is your name?" His voice trailed off.

"Now why would the great Mr. Ebenezer Scrooge want to know the name of some poor, lonely, street rat?"

Awestruck at how much she bore the likeness of Belle, he remained silent.

"In case you haven't already figured it out, I will spare the unnecessary suspense," she answered immediately. "You and my mother were to be married."

Her chin was high, and one eyebrow raised toward him skeptically.

"Gracious me!" Ebenezer tilted his body against the brick wall and loosened the gauze on his throat, staring at her in disbelief. Her lips had the same natural flower-petal pink color as Belle's did, and her shapely eyebrows arched upward at exactly the same angle. His mind was racing with so many questions at such a speed, that it was impossible to settle on a single one.

"Of course that was before the money, right?" she asked spitefully.

"I…"

"You fell more in love with your money than you did with her. Remember?"

She looked to be in her mid-forties, but her countenance and body language came across as if she wasn't a day older than twelve.

Ebenezer shook his head and continued to make unintelligible sounds while he stammered for words.

"So, in answer to your question, my name is Melody. Humorous," she smirked. "She described you as a tall, dark, handsome, and strong man with the world on a string around your neck."

"She...She said these things? To you?"

"The man I see is nothing more than an old, shrunken, pathetic, penny-pinching weasel in mummy wraps. I'm ashamed to know that my mother could have ever loved you."

Her words were delivered in a girlish and immature manner that did not match her grown-up, lovely, and dignified face. Her low-class accent—a trait she most certainly did not inherit from her mother—matched those of the beggars in London's gutters.

She struck him as an overgrown child attempting to intimidate him. It was sad.

Ebenezer opened his mouth to speak, but couldn't find the words.

"At least I can be proud of her for leaving you, though her reasoning seems a bit desperate now that I look at you up close. All she wanted was to be cherished, so she left."

"I never meant...I would have never..."

"Spare me your ramblings old man, I'm not the idiot that she was."

If all intellect hadn't completely escaped him, he would have scolded her for ever speaking of Belle in such a way. Now though, he couldn't form a decent sentence if his life depended on it. Too much was happening too fast, and it didn't look like this woman, this...beautiful daughter of Belle's, was going to stop long enough for him to catch up.

"Nevertheless, for whatever reason, she told us about you, her first love."

Ebenezer felt tears welling up in his eyes. He would have thought that he had cried his tear-well dry in the past few days. Apparently, that was not the case.

"Any man in London would have given their life for a single smile from her direction, but you?" She shook her head, sighed, and then leaned casually into the wall to face him even more directly. "Her voice couldn't compete with the jingle of your purse."

"No, I…"

"Her hair would never be shinier than the gold in your safe, would it?"

"That's not the way it was."

"Yes it is," Melody snapped at him hatefully. "She became so weary of comparing herself with your wealth, she left you for someone else!"

At this, Ebenezer looked into her eyes with sudden urgency.

"Was he good to her?"

Melody looked confused by his reaction, as if she was expecting jealousy, not concern. Lifting her weight from the wall, she took a deep breath, and looked beyond him, into a blur of hazy bricks.

"No," she said with contempt, satisfied that she had another opportunity to lay the blame on Ebenezer. "He hurt her."

Ebenezer shook his head angrily. "No, no, how could anyone hurt her? Who would…"A salty fugitive tear slipped onto the skin of his cheek and soaked through the wrappings, causing a mild sting.

"She was never the same after she left you, and the years that followed were worse. Of course he was nice in the beginning…They all are." She stared at him pointedly.

"What happened?"

"Why the concern after all these years, Great-and-Mighty Scrooge?"

"Tell me what happened, I beg of you."

Melody glared at him skeptically, her pretty eyes narrowing to slits. "He found his drug of choice, and never had a sober moment afterward. He was abusive to all of us, and gambled away our money, our furniture, our livestock, our home, our land...Then he was involved in a horrible accident that took his life."

Ebenezer's eyes were full of pain. He realized that this woman had just come from out of nowhere, and with her intent thus far seeming completely vengeful, he had no reason to believe her words, especially how easily it had been for her to tell him these things. However, *because* he did not know her, he had no reason not to believe her. She was opening up extremely fast to someone she hated. Ebenezer's only guess was that she had been planning this moment of revealing her agony for quite some time. Now she looked as if she felt cheated, after such a time of dreaming up the confrontational moment that would finally bring her face to face with her mother's biggest mistake, ready to defend her at any cost, only to be met with an old, repenting fool. Sighing, she continued.

"We were almost relieved when he was gone, so he couldn't be there anymore to hurt her. We of course lived happier with no fear or abuse, but with absolutely nothing. He was gone, but not until he had been on the earth long enough to rob us of all we had. What little we did have left had his filthy, wretched mark all over it, including heavy debts with the wrong kinds of gambling acquaintances. Once he was gone, they came to my mother to collect."

"Good heavens! Tell me no more!" Ebenezer wept. "No, I need to know. Please, go on..."

Seeing the agonizing effect her story had on him seemed to be an unexpected blessing for her. He knew she truly hated him and wanted him to suffer as they had.

"When did this happen?" he asked through stifled sobs.

"Years ago." Melody bent down and retrieved his cane from the ground, slowly spinning it in her fingers and studying the hand-carved craftsmanship. He knew that to her, it represented the kind of things he spent his money on while living in the lap of luxury.

"Then, months ago, mother got sick."

Ebenezer cradled his arms to his chest.

"My siblings and I were suddenly threatened with losing the only thing that still gave our miserable lives any happiness." She sighed, threw his cane down again, and shook her head. Her beautiful curls had fallen in front of her face, and she made no attempt to brush them aside. Eyes sadly downcast, she continued.

"So one night, my younger brother and I had stepped away from my mother's bedside. We spoke for some time. It was then that we began to hate you, for robbing her of the life she might have had. YOU!" she exploded suddenly. "You stole her chances of being happy!"

"I'm so sorry my dear." Ebenezer shook his head continuously.

"I came close to forgiving you in my heart for pushing her away when you did, knowing that you would have been worse to her and us than our real father."

Melody turned away from him and faced the small groupings of people heading in and out of the shops.

"Until that day."

Looking up from his slouch, he stood, and wandered closer to her. Standing at her side, and looking at her beautiful profile, he waited patiently.

For a while she didn't speak at all. When she finally opened her mouth to continue, her voice trembled with emotion.

"I heard word spread that an old foolish man claimed he was visited by three ghosts, and became a different person. A nice…kind person. I heard the whole story." She continued to avoid eye contact. "I hated you even more when you had apparently changed back into who you were when you first loved her."

Struggling to trap her tears, she took a few quick breaths, and blinked.

"We watched her suffer in many ways throughout the years. She was such a forgiving soul. It was always her will for us also to forgive and forget, but when she fell sick recently…"

"Please," Ebenezer pleaded. "What has become of her?"

Clearing her throat, she wiped her tears away, and adjusted her posture.

"So I came to watch you. You, and your clerk, the well-known city cripple, miraculously saved by the wealth you so mercifully bestowed on him."

Finally she turned on him. Her blond hair whipped around and tumbled against her chest. Her cheeks were flush with anger.

"Let me inquire of *you* now Mr. Scrooge, if I may be so curious. Did precious Tiny Tim do anything to deserve your money? Say oh…promise you his life and love till death do you part? Or is it just that you reserve the right to pick and choose who is and who is not worthy of your kindness and charity?"

"Dear lady, I'm so sorry…" Ebenezer would have given his fortune for all the hurt to go away from this fragile woman. Her frustration was legitimate, and he once again found the wrong decisions of his past haunting his present. Her hurt was more evident moment after moment, making it even harder for him to doubt her story.

"Well, anyway, his majesty Mr. Limp had the keys to your safe and office, so I watched him as well. He saw me out his window once, right after I slipped in and stole the spare key to your office from his nightstand. Judging by his reaction, I guess I frightened him. Not to mention the sight of me in my cloak on the street that night at your window apparently frightened your silly, paranoid mind, and eventually, it became a sport. I had no idea to what extent your imaginations would run, until I slipped back onto the train the day that he had convinced you he was off to buy supplies needed for the office.

"You were there?" Ebenezer's eyes were wide.

"I was at the train station when he boarded for Liverpool. He saw me looking his way, and I ducked out of sight long enough to throw my cloak into my bag, and snuck onto the train after him. I sat down in his car, and he told me he was freezing. I asked him why, and he spared a few details because I was a stranger and unknown to London. He told me about his failing health, and how he was secretly on a mission for a professional and unbiased medical opinion, because he had recent reason to believe that his time was running out. When I asked about it, he simply told me that he had seen something..." She sighed heavily. "It doesn't take a genius to piece the puzzle together. I knew he was talking about the cloaked figure, thinking I was some spirit. That was that."

Giving a decisive nod, she looked away again.

"I rode the length of the trip with him, and when he had arrived, I rode the train directly back here, and disembarked just in time to find you walking alone just before sunset."

"Mercy...It was you all along..." He blinked. "Dear, that night on the street..." He remembered the blade. "Had you the plan to end my life?"

Her answer did not come quickly. She shifted her weight uneasily, and wetted her lips.

"I was tempted."

He stared.

"I have been tempted many times," she admitted.

Ebenezer lowered his brow in thought. "And you were the one that attempted to break in to my safe?"

"Yes." She nodded firmly, and without remorse. "I thought I would try to steal some of our life back. You have so much money, I had concluded that it wouldn't have hurt you to lose most of it. When I stole the key from Tim, it wasn't attached with a key to the safe. As it turns out, I am not much of a picklock."

"Why didn't anyone tell me that any of you were in need?!" He shook his head angrily. "But wait, please…Tell me of Belle! Is she still sick?"

She looked slightly surprised when his anger about the attempted safe robbery never came, and then she appeared as if she felt the smallest guilt for having toyed with him so much.

Ebenezer stood, not daring to breathe.

Melody slowly shook her head, as tears gathered in her eyes.

"My mother is dead."

The world had gone still…

Melody's words filled his head and his heart with a suffocating pressure, and a deep nausea suddenly twisted from the depths of his stomach. The defining edges of all he could see dissolved together, and the sounds around them from the marketplace became like ancient echoes in an abandoned tomb. With all his senses obsolete, he abruptly became dizzy.

Ebenezer fell back against the brick wall once again, in complete shock and unacceptance of her news. Suddenly, his mind ran to thoughts of the days he and Belle were together. He remembered being lucky enough to hold her hand. He remembered her gently climbing onto their buggy to go on picnics and taking her out on social calls with Mr. and Mrs. Fezziwig. Her hand-sewn, dainty dresses edged with lace always framed her elegant form so attractively. When she laughed, her bubbly sound would inspire birds to sing along. There simply wasn't anything about her that wasn't the soul of pure elegance.

Years of agonizing regret and painstaking grief over losing Belle the first time could never hold a candle to how he felt over hearing the details of her possibly preventable death. If only he had known! He could have helped her!

He could now remember the way her hair shone, in and out of the sun, more beautifully than all the gold in the world…

"Well Ebenezer," her voice quivered, wanting to appear unyielding to emotion. "Either you are going to shout for the constable, or I'm going to board the train and begin devising a more intelligent revenge."

At this moment, Melody's dagger would have been much easier to take than her emotional darts, yet he had no right to plead her patience. Ebenezer focused his eyes on her. She was such a beautiful woman, but it was painfully clear she was raging like a storm on the inside, looking much like her mother, but without the untainted happiness. With the details he had just received about their lives, it was evident that Belle's children weren't allowed the innocence that she herself grew up in. The choice to marry the wrong person had cost them all their freedom to live normal happy lives, and the choice to marry the wrong person was more than likely Belle's emotional rebound from a stingy miser's rejection. How selfish he had been.

There was no knowing what kind of hurt they had all been through, and even the thought of abuse of any kind was devastation to Belle's memorial. Her own daughter was pretty as a rosebud, but hard as stone and blackened with hatred.

"Belle was…Your mother was the only woman I ever loved."

Picking his cane up off the ground, he turned it in his own fingers, as if studying it for the first time, and continued.

"I do not blame you for hating me. I am so sorry that my years of selfishness have punished you enough to turn you into this. Please trust that the sight of you this way, in comparison with the memory

I have of your mother then, is revenge enough. My own selfish acts have caused so many people much pain."

Melody scoffed.

"I thought that when I changed, and started doing right, that it would heal the wounds I had inflicted. Now once again, I am accountable for even a higher suffering." Stabbing his cane into the snow again, he glanced out into the street, and back at the woman in front of him.

"Listen to me." Ebenezer's voice cracked. He cleared his throat, and blinked back tears. "I promise, I will make amends." His breathing came faster, allowing his vulnerable desperation to show.

She shook her head. "I don't want amends to be made, Mr. Scrooge. I don't want to be your friend. I don't want to have anything to do with you."

"Except to steal my money?"

She clenched her fists. "DON'T judge me."

"Trust me, money will not give you the things you truly want."

"Neither, Mr. Scrooge, do I want your advice!"

Realizing his mistake, he nodded, paying no attention to the pain after moving his head, and looked to the street.

"My dear, sweet lady, forgive an old fool."

She stood, silently scowling.

"I shall look for you soon. I have the means to help you. I have tripled the fortune your mother spoke of." He started away from her to the main shopping center, once again conscious of his appearance, and pulling his collar high around his neck.

"Dear, sweet Belle. Oh my God…Belle…"

Looking back once at Melody, he pointed his cane toward her and continued sidestepping away.

"I…I will come for you. Or you can come back to me. I have no intention of calling the constable or anyone else. Now that I know who and what you really are, there is a very frightened young man I must tend to."

"Walking away, *again*, Ebenezer?" Her eyes glowed a piercing hate that seemed to burn Ebenezer to his very soul.

"I WILL come…I promise."

Chapter Seventeen

What Are You Doing Here?

Anna sat on her knees in the dining room, and called for Marcus to join them. The small pink doily that would be their tea party centerpiece was hand-crocheted by Emily, and had several knots and areas of too much slack, causing it to lie terribly uneven.

"It's beautiful Emily. A finer teapot companion I have never seen."

"Mother taught me to crochet when I was one and a half," Emily said proudly.

"Oh really! That's remarkable!" Anna laughed.

"Yes, an' Marcus will say, 'She's lying!' and he'll make a mean face, but do not listen. He doesn't know about it. It was a secret the whole time."

Marcus entered the room and reluctantly dragged himself to the tea area and sat, disappointed that his game they all agreed to play got cut short when Emily pretended to fall and cry so she could steal Anna's attention.

"Now," Emily began. "Everyone pour yourself some tea because it's very healthy for you."

Anna obeyed, pouring the imaginary tea into her teacup.

Afterward, she brought it to the edge of her nose and took in a deep breath, savoring, smelling, and tasting her cup of air.

"MMMMmmmmmm. This is wonderful tea, Emily."

Marcus jerked the empty teapot and shook it sarcastically over his cup, and then returned it to the middle with a clunk, and drank his imaginary tea down in one exaggerated slurp.

"May I go now?"

"In a minute, Marcus. Right now, I would like us to pray."

Until now, the children had only heard their parents talk about prayer, and knew that it meant they had to wait until their parents had their eyes completely closed before they could make faces at one another at the dinner table. However, after seeing their uncle rush by them earlier that day with his face completely covered in gauze, and knowing Tim was missing, the concept of pleading with a higher power to protect and bless had a much more urgent resonance to their young ears.

They bowed their heads and listened to Anna pray. This time, they did not make faces. This was one of many, many prayers they took very seriously within the last few hours. Silently in their heads, they agreed earnestly with every word she spoke.

Before Anna said "Amen," she quieted, allowing the children the opportunity to speak to God personally.

"An' God…" Emily said with her eyes shut tight, "an' help Uncle Ebenezer, an' Tim an'…keep them safe so, an' so until they come home."

"Pray that they will find Tim," Marcus interjected. Anna remained silent.

"An' that they will find Tim an' he will not have, um, bruises."

"Pray that…" Marcus' voice began to tremble and crack. "Pray that they will live, Emily."

"An' help them to stay alive." Emily sniffed. "Please God, an', just make them come home so, an' be happy an' be safe."

Anna cried silently while they prayed, not allowing them to hear her weakness, wiping her tears away with her tea party handkerchief. She was glad the children had their eyes closed.

"Pray that they will drive safe."

"An' so they won't fall off the cart an'..."

Bob paced back and forth in Mr. Scrooge's office. He had looked everywhere he could think of, and some places were checked twice. He was beginning to panic himself into a corner.

"I...I...I should have told him."

He didn't know whether to stay there, in case Tim chose to go to the office, or wander out and attempt to find him again on the streets somewhere...Then again, if he was out on the streets somewhere, it was bad news, bad news...

"Should have let him see your letter while I had the chance, Margaret!"

He nervously poked the fire.

"Should have...should have..."

The quill was in the wrong place. It needed to be on the left side of the desk. No, on second thought, it looked better on the right.

"Margaret love, what's...what's going to happen to our son?"

Come to think of it, the quill wasn't the problem. It was the parchment of all things! It needed to be centered!

"He's going to live, right? I mean, I mean, he's going to live, *right?*"

No, this wouldn't do. It wouldn't do at all. The candle needed to be right next to the reading glasses, and the inkwell should never be placed that close to the edge! Why was NOTHING in this blasted office organized!?

Bob fell to his knees and hugged himself in a fetal position.

"Get a hold of yourself doctor..."

. . .

Dr. Webber tossed his medical bag to the ground atop a suitably fluffy pile of snow. Gripping the edge of the carriage, he slid his weight carefully downward, and steadied himself. Buttoning his overcoat, he lifted his bag and brushed off the excess flakes, and then turned to the ruddy, thick man who had come to fetch him.

"Is this where we find Mr. Scrooge?"

"To be honest sir, I don't know. He is usually here, though with everything the way it has been lately, I can't be sure."

The doctor smiled respectfully. "Well, from what it appears, you have already fulfilled several unexpected and lengthy duties. I will be fine to locate him here on my own."

"Thank you, sir," he replied, eager to return home. "When you do find him, please tell him that I would like my own cart and horses back as soon as he finds time to return them."

"Of course."

Dr. Webber lent a sober wave to their parting. Even though he had no idea why he was sent for, he had a horrible feeling that it had something to do with his diagnosis of his old student's son several days earlier, and he was ready to defend his expert opinion, as sad as it was.

He was as professional as professional could be, with years of knowledge and training in medicine, and he only had one rule. He would never lie to his patients. It was their life, and they deserved to be told the truth, even when the truth was sorrowful. Little Tiny Tim of Mr. Scrooge's shop was sadly no exception.

Taking a deep breath and straightening his hat, he walked a few steps and rapped his knuckles on the door, just under the gold panel with "Ebenezer Scrooge" embossed in heavy scripted letters.

Scarcely had he stopped his knock, when the door was thrust

open, and Bob Cratchet stood behind. His expression went from hope to confusion.

"Dr. Webber?"

"Dr. Cratchet...I didn't expect to see you here."

"Your presence is quite a surprise as well. What are you doing in London?"

He smiled warmly, and swallowed. "Mr. Scrooge sent for me by name."

"What would...Uh, I'm sorry, I have forgotten my manners. Do come in."

"Thank you."

The professor made his way in swiftly and laid his medical bag on the seat of the metal hall tree.

"It is good to see you again, Dr. Webber."

Dr. Webber turned around, and shook Bob's hand, all the while continuing to remove his hat and loosen his scarf. "And you as well, my good friend."

Under other circumstances, this reunion would have been happily born. But after an awkward moment, it seemed that both men, for different reasons, were nervous about what the other might say.

"I...uh...I apologize if I don't appear in a merry mood," Bob began. "You see, I had just happened by, and I thought you may have been someone I was hoping might have shown up. We have been...There have been..."

Bob started his jerky pacing again and awkwardly fumbled with his hair, his buttons, his pockets...

Dr. Webber felt for his peer, but was at a loss for words himself.

"Why are you here, Dr. Webber?"

He nodded in response. "Yes Dr. Cratchet, perhaps that is the best place to start. Would you care to sit?"

Chapter Eighteen

What Might Have Been

After too much running, too little food, and too many hours of shivering, Ebenezer was legitimately exhausted. His entire head burned, throbbed, and itched miserably, and he had thought several times that he might have passed out from the pain already. He felt lost and defeated standing there in the icy wind with nothing but a pure saturation of bad news and impending danger for days now.

His only consolation was the fact that at least Tim wasn't going to be carried away by the grim reaper. Now that the confusion of the ghost had been cleared up, it was just a matter of that blasted doctor and his malpractice of jumping to conclusions. Being free and clear of a ghost wasn't much of a prize though, against the possibilities of Tim getting into trouble by overreacting to false spirits, and with Tim being nowhere to be found, that *was* a possibility. Nobody had even reported seeing him. Of course, nobody seemed to recognize Ebenezer wrapped up in layers of crazy medical nonsense, so he couldn't blame anyone if they had been dishonest about having seen Tim.

He took a few reluctant steps with no particular direction in mind. Sighing heavily, he once again weighed his options.

By this time, Bob or Fred may have found Tim, and the three of them could be in a safe place, talking quietly over a hot mug of pudding. If he gave up the search now, he may find out later that just the next place he would have thought to look would have been Tim's hiding place. Then he would have to live with the regret of discontinuing his search, yet another selfish decision, and at this very moment, there was no way of knowing what kind of danger Tim might be in.

Throwing up his weary arms, Ebenezer stopped. He had simply had enough of the wretched gauze. Beginning at the top, he ripped the cream- and puss-soaked wrappings and unraveled them from his face. His skin had barely begun to attach itself in certain areas, and he gritted his teeth and cried out in pain as the soft membrane tore.

Several agonizing minutes later, he realized that it might have been a good thing to let his skin breath. The soft, cool snow hit his skin openly, soothing it for the moment. Still in a great deal of pain, he somehow sensed that giving up wasn't an option. Yet he knew he couldn't force his old body in its current condition to go on much longer unless he catered to himself with warm food and dry clothing.

Regretting his earlier decision to leave the cart behind for easier crowd travel, he set forth on foot into the middle of the street from the alley. Not many people were out, which was odd, even for late in the afternoon.

Suddenly, Ebenezer felt hazy and short of breath.

After briefly combing the area, he spotted a little girl reaching on her tiptoes to flip the sign of a toy store from "open" to "closed." Moments later, a lanky older gentleman stepped outside the store and began fumbling with his keys.

"Excuse me. Old man," Ebenezer said without concern for proper title. "Why are you closing the store? It's not evening yet."

Speaking aloud caused him to wheeze.

The man turned, squinted, and upon closer look at the raw-skinned, cane-clutching hunchback heading in his direction, turned his key and smiled politely.

"All the shops close early on Christmas Eve, sir. Have a splendid holiday."

Upon his last words, the man rushed into the door, grabbed his little girl around the waist, and headed into the back room hastily blowing out candles on the way.

"Christmas Eve? Christmas EVE!?" Ebenezer repeated. "I suppose I *have* been pre-occupied. Bah! Infernal stingy businessmen… Wretched hooligan shopkeepers blowing out candles on poor helpless old men in the streets…nowhere to go…no food…no dry clothing…no *skin*…"

He looked about, seeing only closed businesses in every direction, and decided to head to the next cross street in hopes of some poor fool attempting to make a few last Christmas sales.

"I can't believe tomorrow's Christmas! How could I forget?" he said to himself. "I never even knew!"

His steps started to slow. Nausea crept into his upper stomach.

"What a lousy Christmas this will be. Eh spirits? Funny thinking of how times have changed, isn't it?"

His voice sounded weak, even to himself.

"And by the way spirits, where are you now?"

Reaching the next street, he looked both ways to see complete desertion. He felt an unfamiliar trickle on his cheek, and reached to touch it.

"Now that…" His breath caught in his throat, causing a few heavy coughs. "Now that everyone else is gone."

Bringing his fingertips in front of this face, he saw that it was blood-splattered. Ebenezer closed his eyes, tempted to keep them closed. The sight of his own blood on his hand made him feel a bit faint. Apparently it was not a wise thing to remove his wrappings.

"Eh?" He breathed long and slow breaths. "Where are you now?"

Stopped in the middle of the street, he blinked, blood from his forehead filling his eyes.

"Shoulda…kept that eye…closed I suppose."

Lightheaded and disoriented, he raised his eyes to the street again. With shock setting in, suddenly he couldn't remember why he was there or where he was headed. All he could focus on was the excruciating pain as his whole body pulsed from head to toe.

"The snow is…pretty out here…Shoulda left the…medical… on, I suppose."

A sharp pain shot through the top of his head with the weight of a wood splitter, starting at his forehead and ending at the brain stem.

"I'm bleeding…somebody help."

Crying at barely a whisper, he dropped to his knees, then felt his full body weight crumble forward in a plop. While on the ground, he could see the blood that had collected in the collar around his numb neck trickling onto the white snow.

He fought to remain conscious.

"Help me somebody."

The iciness from the ground beneath him crawled into his chest. He could feel his heart beating irregularly, all the while only sure of one thing… *This was not a dream.*

"Spirits…help me…"

As his body was flat on the ground, he strained to see a small pair of shoes appear from beyond a distant wall with characteristic little-boy spats, which climbed into a perfectly fitting tuxedo. As the small child drew near, Ebenezer thought he recognized him.

"Jack? Is that…you…my boy?" he asked weakly between breaths.

"Yes sir! 'Tis I! In the flesh!...Sort of."

Ebenezer smiled. Even though a part of him questioned the child's convenient timing, the sight of anybody brought relief.

"Get...help..." Ebenezer waved his hand fraily to shoo the boy away. "Go..."

Jack approached quickly, clumsily kicking a few loose snowflakes into Ebenezer's eyes, and held out his hand.

"Here, Mr. Scrooge, take my hand."

Ebenezer blinked the snow from his eyes, and stared in disbelief.

"Take your...hand?"

Jack smiled sweetly, and put his hand several inches closer.

"Take it. Take my hand."

A few deep coughs later, he blinked and felt his body relaxing into the soft snow. He was going numb anyway, so the icy bite from the ground was dissipating.

It would only be moments before drifting into the comfortable state of unconsciousness. He thought about Jack. What an odd and mysterious child he was. From the very beginning, he had come from out of nowhere, and had a history of doing exactly that. Nobody that Ebenezer knew had any personal encounters with him, and all the while he spoke with him, he was unable to figure out where he had seen him before.

Looking at the hand in front of his face, he noticed something odd. There appeared to be almost a complete lack of flesh tone. Following up the boy's arm to his face revealed that the boy now appeared in complete shades of peachy-gray. Strangely enough, he wasn't at all frightening.

"What are you?" he asked wrinkling his forehead weakly.

"Mr. Scrooge," the boy repeated, staring the old man in the eye. "Trust me. Take my hand."

It was strange. Ebenezer felt drawn in. It was similar to the feeling he had when a voice told him to awaken the night before. Not the inability to make his own decision, but the sensation to move forward with something that he trusted but didn't understand, because it felt safe. When Jack said to trust him, somehow, oddly, he did.

Summoning his last ounce of energy, he lifted his ice-cold hand from the ground, and placed it into Jack's.

It happened in moments.

Upon contact, Ebenezer felt a powerful heat grow in his palm. It moved gently throughout his hand, into his fingertips. Inch by inch, his arm, shoulder, and eventually his chest were filled with the thickest, most robust radiance.

Areas of numbness that had filled his body moments before returned to fullness of feeling, and without the searing pain.

Seconds later, his body felt more free of age and discomfort than he could remember ever feeling, even in younger years.

His eyesight was perfectly clear for the first time.

It was as if someone, or something, had taken all the wonderful things in the world; human kindness, harmony, laughter, memories, dreams and fantasies, hot cocoa, puppies at Christmas, and joy, and had injected it into Ebenezer Scrooge's bloodstream. Taking in a deep breath, he felt as if he were floating above the world as free as a bird.

A sweet serenity crept in, offering a refreshing peace to his very soul, like a deer panting for water, tasting the cool crispness of a trickling brook for the first time in days. The very air that he breathed was the cleanest, coolest, and freshest he had ever inhaled.

"Stand up," Jack said.

Obediently, he raised himself from the ground.

"Am I healed?"

Jack released his hand and smiled once again.

"Nope, 'fraid not. Your physical body is still in absolutely terrible condition," he said shaking his head and gazing at the ground. "It's gonna hurt so bad later."

Ebenezer looked down, and his body lay next to his feet, blood here and there, and skin melted from the collar bone to his hairline, mostly on the left side. Huge sores still trickled fluid. The sight of himself looking even worse than when he had first been burned startled him.

He no longer found it a wonder that people were afraid of him. *He* was afraid of him. Releasing Jack's hand, he knelt down and touched the hand of his own body, and flinched back. It was almost as stiff and cold as a corpse.

"Am I…Am I dead?"

Jack turned his gaze to the body on the ground. "No, not yet. You are dying though, Mr. Scrooge. You should have died twice now if you consider the incident at the fireplace. Somebody up there is protecting you. I guess He's not through with you just yet."

"He?"

"Yep."

Ebenezer shook his head in bafflement. His thoughts raced with hundreds of questions all at once.

"Are you real?"

"No. In one sense, I don't exist. But on the other hand, I have been around long enough to know everything about you." Jack nodded, as if this had been a perfectly understandable answer.

Ebenezer ran his fingers through his now clean, thick hair, perplexed.

"Am I hallucinating?"

"Wrong again."

In this present out-of-body state, where everything felt wonderful, he was unwilling to feel impatient or angry. He simply stood confused and silent.

Jack laughed aloud. "It is fortunate that you called for help when you did."

Ebenezer turned his gaze back to the child. He studied his young features, still unable to place where he had seen him, and finally narrowed down the spinning wheel of questions to one.

"Jack... Will I ever know who or what you are?"

The young boy returned his stare with an understanding smile.

"One day, Mr. Scrooge, you will know everything. Right now though, there is only so much you are allowed to know as long as you still inhabit the earth."

The boy still spoke like a child and looked like a child, but it was clear that his knowledge of the things beyond the physical world was astounding.

"You still have absolutely no idea who I am?"

"No, I do not. You have looked familiar since I first saw you, but I don't know who you are." Ebenezer looked at his surroundings. Still in the middle of the street, in the early evening hours, daylight had just begun to dwindle, and his physical body was bleeding to death on the ground nearby. He was bewildered, and almost literally speechless. Not knowing where to start, he simply looked back at the boy and shook his head in puzzlement.

"Allow me to introduce myself. I am the Ghost of Christmas That Never Was. Come with me, Mr. Scrooge. I will show you things you need to know."

Jack turned, and as boyish as ever, lightly skipped down the street about half a block.

Ebenezer followed behind, without strain.

The surroundings began to fade away slowly, and form into a tunnel made of swirls of every color in the rainbow. A vast array of twisting light patterns and flashing cloud-like designs meshed together in one bewilderingly beautiful pattern. It was certainly nothing the earth would have been able to produce. This was an amazing place, with a strangely familiar feeling, although Ebenezer was one hundred percent positive he had never even dreamed of it.

Overhead and all around, large bubbles opened up, portraying emotional scenes of various gatherings and the love, hatred, loneliness, laughter, of families Ebenezer would never know.

"Who are these people?"

"They are simply portrayals of what never was but may have been."

"What? What do they have to do with me?"

"They might have been your memories, of people you may have met."

Ebenezer started to become dizzy and confused, but waited patiently.

Eventually, Jack stopped, looked in a specific direction, as if studying something behind the curtain of bending hues.

"You have been visited before. Sixteen years ago, they came to help you change, and be a better man. That is not why I am here. I have come to help you understand what you have become, so that you may no longer be a slave of the never-ending question of what might have been."

Ebenezer heard his name spoken gently, and slowly allowed his eyes to drift to a nearby bubble. An old schoolteacher was helping the small Ebenezer out of a puddle. Then the image faded.

Jack continued. "You are useless to your purpose, caught in a negative whirlpool of possibilities that are so endless you can never experience them all, or expect to know what they could have led to. You have analyzed yourself into a state of paralysis. Do you understand?"

Taking his eyes away from a bubble of an extremely old and decrepit Ebenezer choking on a pill at his bedside, he nodded initially, and then closing his eyes from the disorienting surroundings, muttered a small "no."

"To be honest, I'm not sure I would have understood it much myself if the Boss hadn't explained it to me. However, I was willing to memorize it and say it as good as I can." Jack giggled.

"Your boss? I am even more confused. For whom do you work?"

"You may open your eyes now, Mr. Scrooge."

It was as if time stopped completely. Everything Ebenezer saw was now black, as if he had been pulled into a void, into another dimension where no life at all had ever existed.

"Where are we?"

"This is the place where all possibilities are stored. Events that *did* occur, events that *did not* occur, and even records of events that *will never* happen…"

"I…I see."

"When you were visited before, you were taken to the past, present, and possible future. This is simply where all of the past, present, future, and 'never-was' exist. Everything can be viewed from here. The Boss created this place for occasions just like these, and people just like you."

Jack held his hand in the air, palm up, and a giant, beautifully painted picture with a gorgeous and complex solid gold frame appeared. It portrayed two men, one with his arm on a woman's shoulder. The two men were Marley and Scrooge, at a young age. The woman was Belle. They were standing in the snow, under a large tree. Belle's face was very forlorn, the other two seemed careless.

"Take a look, Mr. Scrooge."

When Ebenezer began to truly focus on the picture, the images began to move. The canvas came completely to life. As he watched, a gentle tugging at his skin began at his cheeks, and then with sudden force, sucked his body in. The very next second he found himself crouched behind a bush with Jack, watching the scene unfold first-hand.

"Ebenezer my love, why can't you spare a few more shillings a week at least? His family will starve!"

The young Scrooge in the picture scoffed at Belle and turned proudly to Marley. Marley laughed in return.

"Perhaps his family's hunger will persuade him to scribe faster, my dear."

Belle looked heartbroken and helpless.

"Put yourself in his shoes, darling. Imagine that I am at home with my children, starving to death because you work for two misers who won't pay you half of what your labor is worth. What would you do?"

"Listen wife, you are the one that dragged me and Marley to this silly party of your father's, and—"

"But the Fezziwig's Annual Christmas Ball is the most important day of the year for Father!"

"Silence! I was NOT through…"

"No," Ebenezer said. "There's no way I could have ever been that insensitive to her!"

"Shhh…listen, this part is even worse!" Jack said with a childish grin.

"—and instead of allowing me to at least hate being in the assembly inside where it is warm, you insist on dragging me and my business partner out in the snow to play silly 'what-if-it-were-you' games. The facts are, I don't *work for two misers, you're* not *starving, we* don't *have children because I hate them, I* am *cold, I* am *irritated, and I want to go inside. Now!"*

Once Scrooge had put his foot down, he turned to Marley, smoothed out the front of his overdone tuxedo, and cleared his throat.

"Come Marley, let her remain outside and cry all night if she chooses. I'm going inside to loathe this deplorable fiasco from the warmth of the fire."

Belle watched as they left, falling to her knees in the snow, miserable, alone, and completely disrespected.

Slowly the image went still once again, leaving the haunting portrait of Belle on her knees weeping. Ebenezer and Jack were lightly lifted back out of the frame.

"This is trickery! I will not believe it!"

"I know," Jack agreed. "It's hard to believe. Nonetheless, this was a brief glimpse into exactly the way life would have been if you had actually married her when you were partnering with Jacob Marley."

"No." Ebenezer shook his head. "I would have never been such a monster to her."

Jack giggled and waved his hand upward, obliterating that picture from existence.

"I know what you mean. I thought you were a right pig to her in many of the possible realities that I have viewed. Imagine if she had actually married you. At least with her true husband, she had her children. She lived for them in fact. But you wouldn't have had them at all because you hated children, just like you hated me when we met."

"Thank you Jack, for always being so tactful and discreet with your observances!"

"I take after my father in that regard." Jack lifted his palm to the black nothingness, and another picture appeared.

"Watch, Mr. Scrooge, yet another possibility."

It was a picture of a hand-carved wooden table with a silver woven cloth covering, Belle on one side and Scrooge on the other, and nothing but the tiniest half of a baked ham in between them, a lousy companion to such a finely decorated dining room. Luxuriant blue velvet curtains cropped the window behind them, and small holly plants were scattered about.

Ebenezer focused on the picture, and allowed himself to once again be pulled in to a flash of what might have been.

Standing only inches away from her beautiful face, he was tempted to reach out and touch her.

"You did the right thing, Ebby love. Marley was a terrible partner."

"You realize of course that this means a great cut in our lavish lifestyle? So many things we will have to go without. Our Christmas this year will be almost nonexistent."

Belle smiled warmly, and began cutting the tiny ration of meat.

"My love, they are just things. *Nothing more. I would rather go without pretty dresses and silk linens, and know that you will have nothing to do with that morally bankrupt Mr. Marley, than to live rich in possessions but have to pray for my husband's redemption on a daily basis. That man is no good for us. All he thinks about is money, and he doesn't care who he has to trample on to attain it."*

"He is a powerful man. I fear he will own all of London someday, and when our payments are due, he will be a ruthless enemy."

"How much would our payments weigh on a scale, against our happiness?"

Ebenezer had to hold back tears. He could not believe she was truly gone. What a wonderful woman she was.

Belle slid the plate over to Ebenezer. "You haven't eaten anything all day. Please eat, my love."

His eyes scanned the plate, and he shoved it back.

"I have no appetite."

Belle smiled patiently, walked to the other end of the table, and supportively put her arms around him.

"We will make it on what we have, because we will have us."

Ebenezer fell slowly into her embrace. "I know."

The picture slowly faded. They had returned to blackness once again, leaving a young Ebenezer and Belle hugging in a still portrait beside them.

"Why couldn't I have had that life?" He sniffed, gazing at Belle's image. "We wouldn't have needed money if we would have had each other."

Jack shrugged, and patted his friend on the back.

"Come now Mr. Scrooge, there is more to see."

"Wait..."

"Yes?"

Ebenezer paused, and tried to shake the sense of guilt that was now creeping back up to his gut. "I saw her daughter today." Looking down at Jack, he shook his head. "She hated me, Jack."

Sadness toyed with the edges of the small boy's features.

"Her hurt was so deep, and I felt that it was my fault. So many selfish decisions are made early on that affect everything and everybody."

"Now I see what the Boss meant."

"What do you mean?" Ebenezer wiped away a single tear.

Jack stepped back toward the portrait, and wiped it from the universe.

"This never-ending vortex you're in. You're drowning in the sorrow you have for the things you have done. That, of course, blinds you to your life's purpose, and you can't step forward to do the things that you need to do for fear of wrong decisions that may affect others as well as you. Take, for example, your nephew's offer to reside in his home."

At this, he suddenly stiffened.

"You claim to know so much about me, yet you act as if it wouldn't be selfish for me to pull my family into the constant state of unrest that I currently live in."

"Ah..." Jack said, beginning to pace in his mini-tuxedo on the ground of nothingness. "You are assuming you're the only one who lives in a constant state of unrest. What about Fred? Did you not see the reaction he had when he saw your latest injury? Do you think he goes to bed at night without burden? Constantly wondering if the next day will be the day he receives the dreadful news that you will no longer be around to play with the children? And what about the children? Do you know when or how often they cry for you? Is it possible that they might have to grow up faster than they should because they are more aware of what you deal with than you realize? Children are smarter than you know. They are well aware of your situation, and the weight they feel is substantially heavy."

"You expect me to believe that they spend all their time moping around about me?"

"See for yourself."

Jack flipped his palm, and a picture appeared of Fred next to Ebenezer on the floor in his guest room.

"I remember that night. That was only about a week ago!"

Ebenezer slid into the picture, and stood with Jack, watching from the hallway. The old man struggled to break free from his tangled blankets, and then rose up to tell Fred about his dream. He spoke of how his feet were hot and he was being pulled into the earth suffocating, and then asked his nephew what he thought the dream might mean.

"I think it means..."

"Yes?"

"That you wear one too many pairs of socks at night, and you manage well at wrapping yourself into suffocating knots."

Then freeing one hand and pulling some more slack at the neck of his blanket, he cleared his throat.

"You don't believe that it can have meaning?"

"Jack, why are you showing me this? I remember it well."

"Just watch."

Fred stood and offered his uncle a helping hand. Several minutes of untangling commenced, followed by a pat on the back, and an exchange of goodnights. As the door to the guest room clicked shut, Fred blew out the candle in hand, and set it on a corner table.

Ebenezer moved against the wall, and watched. Fred seemed entirely oblivious to his other-dimensional viewers.

The smile on his face faded. Staring down the empty hallway, he allowed his weight to tilt against the wall as he ran his fingers intensely through his hair. Rubbing his eyes hard, he then locked them on the back of the door that his uncle slept behind. Silently, he sighed.

Whispering a quick prayer, he then moved down the hall. A thin bedroom door opened on the way. Emily emerged, holding tight to her blanket, and looked up at her father.

"No no no no, go back to bed," Fred intervened immediately. "What do you want? A drink of water? I have heard it all from you tonight, now turn around and go back—"

"But, what about Uncle Eb?"

Her eyes were sincerely concerned. It wasn't simply the excuse to get out of bed that Ebenezer was expecting. The legitimate fear on her small face was heartbreaking.

"He's fine. He just fell off the bed. He's perfectly fine now okay?"

Fred scooped his little girl up in his arms and entered her bedroom.

Laying her gently down on the bed, he kissed her forehead and pulled her blanket up to her neck.

"But...But what if, this one time, he falls off the bed and hits his head really hard, or somebody doesn't know that he's hurting?"

Fred obviously didn't know how to respond.

"Sweetheart, go back to sleep now. Try not to worry about Uncle Eb. He will be just fine. Okay?"

Emily sighed. "Okay, but what if, this one time—"

"Shhhh...Don't worry sweetheart. Say a prayer, and it will make you feel better."

Fred kissed her again and left the room.

As soon as the door was closed, a small voice could be heard behind it...

"...an' help him not to choke in the night where nobody hears..."

With a pang of guilt in his stomach, Ebenezer followed Jack and Fred to the other end of the hall, where Lillian stood on her bare feet waiting for his arrival.

"Is he back in bed?"

"For now."

Fred opened their bedroom door and attempted to enter, when Lillian put her arm in the way.

"Did you talk to him?"

"Yes, I did."

"And? What did he say? Will he consider moving in?"

Fred didn't say a word. He just shook his head. Slowly Lillian lowered her arm and allowed him to pass. Reluctantly, he walked into their bedroom. She stayed behind a moment and watched the doors in the hallway. Apparently, Marcus had remained asleep, which was fortunate.

The image went still.

"Well, that's just silly!" Ebenezer took his own turn pacing about on the firm nothing where he stood. "I can take care of myself!"

"Ah yes, fine job you've done of that." Jack made an easy flick of the wrist and the image of Ebenezer's cold, bloodied body on the ground appeared. Three hefty sized sewer rats had already found him and were nibbling and rummaging through his pockets and hair.

Just the sight of the most disease-carrying vermin in London crawling all over his body made his stomach turn. An acidic gurgling welled in his throat, and for the first time since he had left his body, nausea set in. He stared for several moments until he could look at the sight no longer. Turning with a grimace, he faced away from the picture.

"Jack, I have seen enough. Show me what you would have for me to see so I may return. I have many things I must do."

"You are right. Let us hurry." Jack nodded, and erased the picture with a wave, and then prepared himself to take Ebenezer through the following portals quickly.

Clearing his throat, another picture appeared at Jack's beckoning.

He lead Ebenezer to sit on a bench, just feet away from a young Scrooge and Marley, sharing a sandwich because they were too poor to each have their own, all the while telling silly jokes and planning future business ventures together. They took turns vowing to send their proceeds to the homeless and the fatherless.

In another scene, he saw his great-nephew Marcus killed in an unexpected horse riding accident. He himself did not attend the funeral, because he had money to count.

Yet another picture, Ebenezer got to see one of the happiest moments in some other life, where he, with the help of a few others he didn't recognize, hung a "Now Open" sign on his own poultry shop. Everybody clapped and sang, "For he's a jolly good fellow."

In another possibility, a scene played wherein the Cratchet family was healthy and happy from the beginning, because Bob had never seen the opportunity to be employed by Mr. Scrooge, and someone saw his potential, and invested in his early medical training.

One picture after another. Some happy, some sad, some plausible, nearly realistic, and some that seemed to be fragments of either very bad, or very good dreams.

Ebenezer was completely baffled. It was amazing how one small decision could alter entire lifetimes of everyone and everything. The possibilities were literally limitless, and just the concept of being responsible for all conceivable paths of life was boundless and immeasurable. Only *contemplating* an idea like that was enough to make his head spin.

"There is one more thing I would like to show you, Mr. Scrooge, that will help you understand why I came to you the way I did."

"Lead on spirit. I have been anxious to understand much about you."

Jack prompted the last picture. An enormous Christmas tree sat in front of a giant window. Belle sat with a small dog on one chair, and a forty-year-old Mr. Scrooge sat on the other side.

Once inside the picture, Ebenezer stood with Jack next to the fireplace.

"Thank you for the coffee, my dear."

"You're welcome."

"You look lovely this morning."

"And you always look handsome, my love."

Mr. Scrooge smiled and sipped from his mug. Belle stroked the little dog in her lap, and then turned her attention to the hallway.

"What do you suppose is taking so long?"

"I don't know. He is late this year, isn't he?"

Suddenly, footsteps could be heard from the end of the hall. Mr. Scrooge threw his head back and laughed. "Here he comes."

The footsteps started off slow, and then in an instant, bolted in a flurry of small pitter-patters, toward the room where they were gathered.

"Merry Christmas mum! Merry Christmas pop!"

Ebenezer held his arms out, and caught the little boy mid-jump, and held him close.

"Merry Christmas Jack!"

Belle laughed aloud at his excitement, and waited in line for her own Christmas greeting.

"Jack…" Ebenezer looked down at the little Jack by his side. They were identical outside of their clothing. The Jack in his father's arms was in his pajamas.

He looked between the two of them, and then back to the one at his side.

"You…my son?"

"I appeared to you in the form that I knew you would be most naturally drawn to. That was the only way you would heed my warnings about Tim."

"Say good morning to your mother, son," Mr. Scrooge said, "and we'll get straight to the presents!"

"Hurry mum, give me a hug!"

Belle embraced him and laughed, then scooted him to the middle of the room.

"Which one first?"

"I don't understand."

"Watch."

Mr. Scrooge rose from his chair and headed into the middle of the room. He knelt down and picked up a medium package, and handed it to Jack.

"I want to start with the most important one son."

"May I?"

"Of course. Go ahead."

Jack ripped it open eagerly, and his eyes grew wide at what was inside.

"Oh Father…" He very gently pulled out several fancy-feathered quills in gorgeous colors, and studied each one, placing them gently on the floor. At the bottom of the package was a small roll of parchment. Jack lifted it from the box, and ran his fingers over its surface.

"Thank you," he said quietly.

"Well, you're welcome m'boy. It's not a lot, but it will at least get you started."

Jack stood, and gave his father a long warm hug. When they had parted, he ran to his mother, who had already begun to get tears in her eyes.

"Thank you both so much. I'm going to write about everything!"

"Go for it m'boy," Mr. Scrooge said.

"I'm going to tell the world about so many things, and they will read it won't they?"

"Ha ha… Of course they will Jack." Belle laughed.

It was difficult for Ebenezer to step out of that picture.

Once back on the outside, he found himself completely speechless. He stared at Jack in bewilderment.

Jack smiled, but his smile was now different. It was almost apologetic. Taking a deep breath, he put his little hands in his pockets, and started to pace.

"I would have been brilliant. By the age of nine I would be reading, writing, and doing unbelievable math."

Ebenezer had a hard time listening. He was still remembering their initial meeting. He just continued to watch Jack pace, and thought.

It made sense to him now why Jack couldn't speak about what his father did for a living, or where he lived. His story about his mother made sense as well, as she was sick and dying at the time. Ironic that the boy reported he was in town to get to know a relative.

It stood to reason why Jack had looked so familiar. All this time however, it wasn't Belle that he looked like. He looked very much like Ebenezer.

"Mr. Scrooge, you would have been impressed with your son."

He stopped in his thoughts, and looked up once again. "A writer?"

"Yes."

"What difference does that make now?" Ebenezer said, trying to understand. "What is the point in showing me all of these things? What relevance does it all have now?"

Jack smiled once again.

"Everything that has happened to you, has affected everyone else, for now. Do you understand that much?"

"Yes."

"You were born and brought into the world to make an enormous difference forever to countless people for years even after you are dead. You were chosen to lead many, well before time began on this earth as you know it, because you are strong. Your story is not one that should go untold. If you had married and had a son, you would have still gone through something similar to your episode sixteen years ago either way. However, in that scenario, your son would have written about it, and your story would live on."

"You try my patience spirit. What difference does that make now?"

"There is another," Jack said suddenly lowering his stare. "He is like a son to you now. You must do all you can to help him. He doesn't know it yet, but the Boss has given him the talent to write beautifully. What happened to you happened for a reason Mr. Scrooge. That story was meant to be told and it must live on."

Ebenezer contemplated Tim. "I must…save him again, right?"

Jack closed his eyes, and opened them again. "In a sense Mr. Scrooge, there's only so much you can do, and it's not entirely up to you to save him. It is partly up to him to save himself, but you must do all you can."

Ebenezer shook his head frustrated. "How? You want me to pay for more doctor bills? Is that my role in this?"

Jack remained patient. "He has given up Mr. Scrooge. He has lost the will to live. The only one who has the ability to reach him is the one who reached out to him the first time. Yours is a strong voice…the only voice he will hear."

Tim.

Ebenezer would do anything for Tim.

When the visitations first came, that was the thing that really changed him. Somehow, for some reason, he always felt a tug toward Tiny Tim.

"Is he really dying?"

Jack let a sad sigh escape from his lips. "His body is weak. Without the will to live, he will die soon."

Ebenezer felt suddenly anxious to go back. So many things revealed to him, and so many new things to think about, yet he knew that neither he nor Tim would last long if he didn't hurry.

"Are you ready, Mr. Scrooge?"

"Yes."

Jack nodded, and held his hand high. He snapped his fingers and a huge cracking sound split the air like a bolt of lightning. The colors instantly came swirling back and more bubbles appeared above them portraying more people Ebenezer didn't know.

He followed behind the small boyish-figured spirit, through all he had seen earlier, in a complete daze. His movements were mechanical as he tried with all of his might to allow some of these new developments to sink in. The trip back was definitely faster than the trip there. The sun was almost down when they arrived where they had begun.

When his feet finally hit the ground near his body, he turned toward Jack. It was harder to look at him now that he resembled the son he literally never had.

Jack stared back, sensing the awkwardness between them.

"Mr. Scrooge," Jack said. "After tonight, no matter what decisions you make, you will not see me again as long as you are alive on earth."

Ebenezer shook his head. "What if I make the wrong decisions sometimes? Who will I…What…"

"You can always repair the things you have broken." Jack smiled and took Ebenezer's hand. With his other hand, he placed something cold and hard into Ebenezer's palm and curled his fingertips around it.

After Jack let go, Ebenezer slowly looked down to his hand to discover the wooden spoon with a ball connected by a knotted string. He instantly choked, and had to wipe away several tears.

He understood why Jack had appeared to him the way he did…but having to part from his son? It was simply a loss he never thought he would face.

Slowly, he regained his composure, held the small knick-knack toy, and sniffed.

"Jack…You said you appeared to me in this form because I would be naturally responsive. Isn't that what you said?"

"Yes."

Ebenezer stood for a moment contemplating.

"What is your true form?"

"I am a messenger. I have had many forms, Ebenezer. You yourself have seen several. My true form will be revealed to you one day, but not in the days that you live on earth."

He was dumbfounded. He couldn't possibly see how he could have missed it before.

"You were the Ghost of Christmas Past, and of the Present, and of the Future!"

Jack nodded.

It was hard to imagine that little Jack was ever as large and loud as the Ghost of Christmas Present, or as frightening as the Ghost of Christmas Future.

"Why have you appeared so many different ways? Why did you time it this way? Couldn't you have just walked into my shop and told me everything?"

"I could have." Jack nodded. "However, as you have learned, the smallest things can mean everything. If I would have simply told you this time, you wouldn't have had the opportunity to bond with what could have been your son, and realize the importance of your relationship with Tim. If I would have just told you everything face to face sixteen years ago, you would have been too stubborn to listen. I have come before you in the exact forms that you needed to see.

"First, appearing as a boy, and then morphing into an ever-evolving form of childhood through adulthood, representing various stages of the past that people have already lived. Second, as a jolly and boisterous soul that thrives on human kindness and joy, representing the things you were lacking at that present time. Thirdly, and most simply, as the fearful fate of your future, lest you change your ways."

It was all too much to take in at once.

"Fourthly, and most importantly, I came to you to help you see that the only thing that matters now is what *IS.*"

"By appearing as Jack…The boy that never was…" Ebenezer smiled.

A moment of silence passed unnoticed, the old man's brain reeling with both comprehension and bewilderment. "A messenger, eh? Was it you who woke me from my nightmare a few nights ago?"

"No, that was not me. That was the one *I* work for."

Ebenezer thought he finally understood who Jack had been referring to as the "Boss."

"But, I don't know Him at all. Why would He speak to me?"

"Ebenezer, continue to read the Book your nephew gave you. I cannot stay long enough to answer all the questions you must have."

He nodded reluctantly. "Will I ever see you again?"

"Yep. But not in this lifetime. However, though you will not see me, until then, I will be in every empty chair beside you."

Ebenezer knew this would be the last moment he would ever have with this entity that had seen him through so many things. This would be his last chance to gather answers that may guide him in the future. His mind raced with so many thoughts he found it hard to focus. He would have to return to his physical body now, and suddenly, though he had many things to do, he didn't want to go. The realization that he would have to go it alone frightened him.

Looking back, his body was motionless and cold.

It had felt so wonderful to be out of pain and away from discomfort of any kind, even for such a short time.

"Ebenezer," Jack spoke. "It is time to go."

"I am frightened to return."

"I know. I know you are afraid. But your body has been strengthened enough to stand up and continue. You must find Tim while he will still hear you."

Tim! Of course Jack would know!

"Yes, Tim! Where can I find him?"

"He is in a place where others have looked, but not seen. This is not the first time that Tim has been missing. You will find him in the same place. It is time…"

"Wait!" he yelped desperately.

"Yes?"

"Please…" Ebenezer's face became so suddenly hopeful, as he clasped his hands together and held them in front of his chest. "Please friend, tell me how to rid myself of my nightmares."

The small boy smiled warmly.

"You have been through much, and you have seen so many things. It is your nature to find the meaning in everything. The secret to ridding yourself is to simply realize they are just dreams. Nothing more."

"But I don't know how to—"

Jack held his hand up, looked down the street, listened, and focused once again on Ebenezer.

"You must go. Time is short."

That was it.

A brilliant light shone, and within seconds, Ebenezer could not focus on him any longer.

Pain erupted into his neck and face, and an icy chill all the way down to the bone marrow gripped his whole body.

He opened his eyes and began wheezing and coughing.

Harnessing all of his strength, he lifted his upper body and pivoted, looking in the direction of where Jack stood.

There was nothing but the empty street, and Jack's small spoon toy.

He pressed his fingers against his skin and saw that the bleeding had stopped. Though judging from the blood surrounding him on the ground, it was a literal miracle he hadn't bled to death or died of hypothermia.

Everything in the last couple of hours had been a miracle.

Grimacing and growling, he pushed his upper body away from the ground just enough to wedge his frozen, worn out leg underneath his chest.

Wiggling one foot flat on the snow beneath him, he finally brought his other leg up, and managed a hunched-over standing.

He looked again where he had stood, moments before, speaking to the angelic little boy. Seeing nobody there, his eyes filled with tears.

He slowly turned to face the brick wall where little Jack had a while earlier appeared from nowhere. His body ached tremendously.

"Jack?...I'm frightened."

There was no answer.

Chapter Nineteen

Nobody's Decision But Your Own

Ebenezer knew that he would not see his small companion anymore. Nobody was there to answer his questions. He realized that he had never felt more alone than at this moment.

Still, he dragged one foot in front of the other, and an inch at a time, brought his hurting, fatigued body toward the next street down. He was only about four blocks away from the square, and his office was just on the other side of that.

His head kept reeling with what Jack had said…"in a place where others have looked, but not seen."

The streets were completely deserted. It was like nothing he'd ever seen. Almost too surreal to be true…Every soul in London had settled in for the night, probably enjoying a hearty turkey dinner with their family. Turkey with mashed potatoes and gravy, and corn on the cob, and hot pudding…Nobody could make hot pudding like Mrs. Cratchet used to.

Ebenezer's stomach churned loudly.

Arriving at the next cross street, he put his weight against a light post and took several deep breaths, still fighting a reckless urge to pass out. Blinking away the stars that appeared behind his eyelids, he flipped his scarf over his shoulder and pressed on.

Step after step, he prodded on to the next street, and the street after that.

Coming to the square, something caught his attention. A small amount of light poured onto the street from a gentle stained glass window in the chapel. The chapel was always open, and at least there would be warmth, and possibly food inside.

Quickening his pace, yet still only moving at a fourth of his normal speed, Ebenezer gained a little more ground with each step. By the time he was at the front door of the chapel, he was elated enough to pretend that he hadn't just hit his knee on the fountain in the square.

Jerking the handle, the doors thrust open easily. Ebenezer dragged himself inside and shut the door behind him.

The inside looked just as beautiful as it ever had, with the addition of holly and tinsel hung around a large elegant nativity scene just inside the door. Though the size of the building was moderate, the majority of the walls within the main room were made up of large arched windows, beautifully stained biblical depictions resembling those on his own fireplace mantle.

There was a calm fire that had been recently stoked, at the right of all the benches.

Nobody was inside, but it wouldn't have surprised him to be joined by a priest at any moment.

At the back of the room was an enormous marble cross that stretched to the ceiling. At its base was a small circular sitting area, casually referred to as "The Prayer Circle" where one could close himself in to light a candle, leave a donation, or pray. It was custom-design, acquired through Ebenezer's contribution a decade before, and it was the congregation's proud claim that it was the only one of its kind.

Looking down toward the middle of the aisle, his eyes landed on the breath of fresh air he had been looking for. He knew very well that the bread and wine had been left out for those who sought to take a private communion, but all things considered, he didn't suppose the Good Lord would mind. There was a good chance that his own money had provided the church with it anyway.

Making his way there quickly, he ripped into the bread and guzzled the wine, which at room temperature tasted like freshly baked bread from the oven with hot tea to his cold bones. He ate and drank so quickly that the wine leaked from the edges of his burnt lips and stung his neck. The pain of the sting was of little concern compared to the growl of his stomach as he continued to devour the food and drink as ravenously as his wounds would allow.

He heard what sounded like a familiar stifled cough from the sitting circle at the bottom of the large marble cross. Ebenezer looked up and thought for a moment…

"… in a place where others have looked, but not seen…"

He would have bet his entire fortune on the fact that Bob or the others had already looked in the chapel, which was Tim's favorite place to go. However, they may have been too frantic to have looked there behind the wall…

Ebenezer's heart jumped.

Walking behind the communion table, he listened hard, staring up at the base of the cross. He thought he heard a faint breath, but he wasn't sure.

He took each step slowly, ascending the steps to the cross.

He heard the definite sound of a second cough.

Creeping to the edge of the circle and peering over, Tim's ruffled hair gave him away immediately.

Ebenezer's heart started racing in his head so loudly it sounded like an overactive metronome in a hollow deerskin drum.

Ebenezer didn't know whether to be excited or angry. It was obvious that Tim didn't care if anyone found him, whether he was officially hiding or not. It was tempting to crawl over the edge of the marble wall and sit with him, but at this point, he thought it better to give him some space.

Mixed emotions toyed with Ebenezer's mind. His heart told him to immediately burst into how much he loved the boy, yet his reason reminded him of how much everyone else had risked to find him. He was here, the whole time, safe and secure in the warmth of the chapel.

What could he possibly say right now that would be unbiased, supportive, and reprimanding all at the same time?

Tim's thin hand-knit sweater was hardly a covering for his skinny body, and the proof was in the way he was shaking. His skin was usually white, but now almost looked bluish. The right leg that sometimes caused a limp seemed to be just slightly contorted at an unusual angle, but for Tim that didn't necessarily mean injury.

"Are you hurt?"

He didn't answer.

He didn't even look up.

It wasn't entirely surprising that Tim knew someone was behind him, but it *was* rather shocking that the sound of Ebenezer's familiar voice was irrelevant. That hurt a little.

"Your family is very worried about you. We've all been out searching."

Still, Tim sat staring forward, offering nothing more than a chesty cough for an answer.

Ebenezer leaned forward a bit, noticing his small friend looked significantly worse than the last time he saw him. Beads of sweat fell from his temples down his cold cheeks. It was unnatural, how his face was completely void of any blush. Even with a fever, there should have been some color in his cheeks.

He suddenly felt pity for him. All selfish running and hiding aside, the young man was miserable, and no doubt felt terribly alone, and with the addition of the recent baby in the house, pressure was added to injury.

Sighing deeply, Ebenezer allowed his weight to shift to the waist-high wall of the marble prayer circle.

"You know, when I was your age, I didn't know love at all. My mother and sister had died, my father had gone away to a debtors' prison from which he would never return, and I had not yet opened my heart to Belle. I had respect for Mr. Fezziwig, but I did not love him the way that you love your family. I wasn't the recipient, in a week, of the love and respect that you receive within an hour."

Tim scoffed, which, selfish as it was, was at least a response. Ebenezer decided that a reproach was not the best way to proceed, so he continued reservedly.

"I know this…When you find love, you need to do whatever you can to keep it, because love and family are all that matter in this world."

He reflected on the last couple of hours, which now felt so far away.

"Heh…I have come very close to death myself, Tim. More than you know."

Still no response.

Ebenezer pulled a cloth from his coat pocket and wiped the sweat from his brow. He was still frozen on the inside, but just being in a heated room with a fire caused him to perspire.

"You must feel lucky to have survived as long as you have, considering what the doctors said when we first took you in, remember?" Ebenezer smiled at the memory of what an amazing recovery he'd had as a boy. "Fresh country air and fish oils, your limbs always splinted or braced…I remember."

Several seconds had gone by and just as Ebenezer was taking a breath to continue, Tim lifted his head. He didn't look directly at his employer, but stared at the beautifully sculpted marble in front of him.

"So that's it, is it? Life is a constant struggle to survive?"

Ebenezer's stomach filled with butterflies when he heard Tim's voice again. He pondered the question for only a moment. Thinking about Belle, her children, his own childhood, his family, Jack's portraits, he was overwhelmed with too many questions himself to feel that he had many answers for someone else. However, with this question he had no doubt. He smiled and responded.

"Well, yes. That is exactly what it is."

Tim sighed.

"Tell me, wise man," he said snidely. "You have many who travel far to consult with you, the spirit-speaker…What is the meaning of all this?"

"What do you mean?"

"Why live at all? You are born, you get sick, you struggle, you break down, you die." At least his angry arm movements stirred up some circulation to his face. "Why do people struggle to survive at all? A silent grave would suffice for me."

Ebenezer's heart both sank and broke at the same time. An extreme sorrow mixed with extreme fear of what could be easily heard as a suicide threat clashed in his soul, causing him to swallow a massive welling lump in his throat. Once again, he patted the sweat from his forehead, and then forcibly cleared his throat before continuing.

"You have more to think about than just yourself now, Tim."

Tim threw his arms up angrily, and remained facing away.

"You are right Ebenezer! I have tenfold the accountability I had as a child. If I would have died then, I would have left the world, leaving behind only my father and mother and siblings!"

Ebenezer thought he saw Tim's face gaining color.

"I may have provided them joy sometimes in exchange for being one more mouth to feed or one more medical bill holding them back from a nicer, bigger home and gifts for the others!

"I may have been terribly young, but I still had to bear the reality of knowing that every event we attended, one member of my family had to stand out from the fun to assist me. Dinner was often bread and water because they had to pay for a new crutch. All of them making constant sacrifices to the tiny cripple in the family!" Tim pulled his knees closer to his body as he yelled.

Ebenezer just stared, blinking at every other word, and allowed him to release his built-up emotions.

"Although it would have caused a temporary sadness to them, my passing then would have only been a blessing! But now?"

He scoffed and shook his head.

"You are right Ebenezer…Now I have a sweet little angel that I have brought into this sickening world, to taste the putrid bitterness of it without a father! I have a wife that I have promised to love and honor until the day I die, which now will come upon us unexpectedly soon! I have to deal with the image of those two precious girls in my head every moment that I have left."

Tim only stopped to take a breath, as he started speaking faster. Ebenezer had opened his mouth to speak words of comfort, but thought that perhaps Tim needed a firmer hand. It seemed comfort would only aggravate him.

"What are they going to do when I'm gone? Are you going to save them with your money?"

Ebenezer sighed heavily and closed his eyes, feeling helpless.

"Can your money buy some wretched freak to replace the void

of husband and father? Not every man has ghostly visitors at the strike of one o'clock flying in to fix everything!"

Even from an extreme side angle, it was obvious that Tim had to try hard not to cry. He continued with growing speed to dominate the conversation as his voice grew louder.

"I wish I had never gotten married, or fallen in love, thinking I would be around long enough for it to be fair to her! I wish I had never brought Margaret into the world just to abandon her, and I wish you would have just LET ME DIE!"

"ENOUGH!" Ebenezer shouted, having heard enough of this self-pity.

A heavy fog of silence filled the room. Tim began to cry quiet sobs, wiping his tears with the sleeve of his sweater. Ebenezer started clumsily pacing outside the perimeter of the enclosed sitting area.

He thought about his earlier visit in the colorful hallway with Jack. Bob Cratchet could have been a doctor early on, and Tim's body might never have suffered how it did.

He stopped, looked at the frail young man, then continued to pace.

His life had affected so many people, and in so many ways. It would be difficult for him to refrain from the temptation of blaming himself for all the world's pain. However, he knew that what he had learned with Jack was substantial. He needed to stop thinking that the world revolved around the decisions he made. It would be just as easy for someone else to have altered his life by the decisions that *they* made.

If there was to be any further redemption for the things he had done, it would rest on what he could accomplish now with Tim. But how could he respond to everything that Tim had just said? If anyone had a heart, they couldn't punish a boy who finds out he's dying after creepy figures have been lingering outside his window. Still, he couldn't stand by and allow him to punish his own family either.

He looked up at the tall, splendidly crafted cross, and marveled. He focused intently for several moments, as if asking for some help. He closed his eyes, said a silent prayer, and then turned his attention back.

"You know, Tim," he began reluctantly. "When the Ghost of Christmas Present led me to your father's house, your father was speaking with your mother. He was telling her why you spent so much time in the chapel. Apparently, he had found you one day, after searching for hours."

He cleared his throat in Tim's silence, and continued.

"When he asked you why you had come here, you said you hoped that people saw you in the church because you were a cripple, and it might be pleasing to them to remember who made the lame men walk and the blind men see."

Tim didn't answer, but his countenance softened a little.

"Well? Was Tiny Tim Cratchet right? Were there people that benefited from seeing your crippled body in a place like this? Have you come to give them comfort again? Have you come here seeking God? What motive has brought Tiny Tim back to the chapel now?"

Tim wiped away a few tears.

"Perhaps I came to confront *my* ghost," he answered sadly, thinking of the cloaked figure.

"Ah," Ebenezer said. "You figured you might as well have it over and done with, eh? No 'goodbye' to the wife and child that you say you concern yourself so heavily with? Just a disappearance?"

"Perhaps. What concern is it of yours?"

"Did you really think to find your ghost of death and darkness here, in a chapel?"

"Maybe I just came to think."

Ebenezer sighed.

"What has happened to you? You have suddenly become 'woe is me' and completely forgotten 'God bless us, every one.' You are fading, Tim. You have assigned your focus to loneliness, physical limitations, and death."

Ebenezer stopped pacing.

"Listen to me. I know what it is to assign your focus to the wrong things. It can alter your future, and everyone else's."

Tim scoffed. "I don't have a future, so what does any of it matter?"

Ebenezer shook his head.

He'd had all he could take. He only ever wanted to be the best friend to Tim that anyone could be. He loved him like a son and would die for him easily, but he was also practical enough to know that sometimes the best thing you can do for a friend is be brutally honest.

"You are feeling sorry for yourself. You have already given up your duties to those that matter most to you, out of fear of the most negative and traumatic conclusion possible."

Tim grew suddenly irritated. "You have still failed, Ebenezer, to explain to me what you have to do with any of this! Why do you feel the need to lecture me about my own decisions?"

Ebenezer felt bitten. "Ah, Tiny Tim. It is as if you have already chosen to die." He stood away from the marble edge and gripped his cane. "And so you shall. I will leave you to it."

He started away from the sad scene and down the stairs. Tim stood and turned, facing the back of the old man's hat and scarves, and shouted.

"You speak as if I am given a choice!"

Ebenezer stopped, but remained facing away. "You are. Why wouldn't you have a choice?"

"I went to see Dr. Webber! Don't you remember? My father is

the greatest doctor in a hundred miles, and he learned everything he knew from him! If he said that I'm dying, I'm as good as dead!"

Ebenezer shook his head and forced himself to speak calmly, raising his focus to the doors of the chapel. "Your father is a doctor, Tim. You're right. And you have heard stories all your life about how the will to live is the most powerful medicine."

"Even if I believed in that jargon, Ebenezer, what of the ghost? Shouldn't you, of all people, regard all the facts in this?"

That was it. Ebenezer turned, facing him irately. "What *of* the ghost?!"

Tim drew back and gasped at the sight of his friend so horribly disfigured with burns. Out of shock alone, he didn't move, cry, or speak, though on the inside, his heart twisted at the sight.

"I once saw my own grim reaper, and I chose that a silent grave would *not* suffice for me!"

He brought his cane down hard against the floor several times as he shouted.

"I was led into the dark future, and watched as they broke into my house after I died and stole my things to pawn off at their illegal fences! One woman even stole the very shirt I was to be buried in from off my body for a few lousy shillings!"

His voice got louder by the second.

"You want to know the facts from me, do you?"

Ebenezer limped a step forward, and then shook his arm so hard, it wiggled his scarf down, revealing more of his charred neck.

"Fact number one! Dr. Webber is a fool who deserves to have his medical license revoked and forced to retire from his practice permanently for how many people his overconfident diagnoses of death must have killed early! It is not Dr. Webber who says when you will die! It isn't spirits! God alone makes the decision of life or death, and if He should choose death, you should die in the arms of your wife!"

Tim's eyes watered. He gulped several times, and pulled his sweater tight.

"Fact number two! Your silly ghost is not a ghost at all! She is just a confused and angry woman, who has been dealt such an unfair hardship that it would make your life look like a bowl of pudding! I met her in the alleyway this afternoon!"

Tim furrowed his brow, confused and still horrified.

"Fact number three! There are many who love you and have suffered greatly for you Tim, and I cannot figure out why you choose to worsen their suffering by being here instead of at home! They are your family!"

Tim hoped sincerely that his best friend's fresh injuries had nothing to do with his selfish disappearance.

"But the choice to be around long enough to deserve their love and love them back is *nobody's decision but your own*!"

Neither of them said a word for several moments. Tim shook his head and bit his lower lip, completely speechless.

Ebenezer gripped his cane, turned, and as fast as his broken body could move, exited from the chapel, leaving Tim to wallow in his own misery.

Ebenezer was glad to see that his office was occupied. He didn't want to bother Mr. Porter this late, and he couldn't be alone for the sake of his health, as he was in need of a doctor badly.

It was strange how as long as he had Tim's whereabouts and safety on his mind, he could continue on through snow, pain, and hunger. Now that he knew Tim was safe, he felt the weight of all his burdens bringing him down fast. How thankful he was that his office was just beyond the chapel.

Falling against the door, he turned the knob, and stumbled in.

"Bob, your son is fine. He is not hurt…or in danger."

Looking into the fire, he felt himself fading as his breath slowed. He had done the best he could at what Jack had asked of him, and now the supernatural strength and power he had been lent was withering.

"I...however...am in great...need of your help."

Ebenezer collapsed.

Chapter Twenty

The End of It All

Daylight was just beginning to break through the icy window, adding radiance to the drab room.

Ebenezer's eyes had been open for several moments now, though his brain had yet to grasp where he was. He remembered collapsing, but couldn't recall why. There was a vague chatter going on in the room somewhere.

His body ached from head to toe, but instinct told him that this was relief compared to the way he felt before he got here.

Books lined the wall neatly on a shelf just below the window. Ebenezer fixed his eyes on the words "Pediatrician's Remedies" before deciding that focusing would lead to nothing more than a massive headache.

Pain shot through his head and he closed his eyes.

The confrontational debate going on somewhere close by began to fade in.

"…telling you, I'm just as qualified a physician as you are, and my son is not dying…"

"…simple as that. He deserves to know the truth, and I'm not the kind of man…"

"…refuse to sit here listening to you speak about the kind of man you are, you simply…wouldn't he have just passed all this time? I for one, don't think you have any right to…"

Ebenezer blinked the dry sting from his eyes, continuing to pick up the fragments of conversation.

"…Bob, this is not just about something your wife told you. This is scientific medical fact, and…he chooses to come to me…will say what's honest, direct…against my professional nature to lie to a patient or lead him on. Tim Cratchet's body did not have the ample medicine in his elementary years to allow for proper development during crucial times…"

"…we taught him to believe in the will to live, and he knows better than to…and I used to think you had all the answers! How could I have been so…"

"…had renal tubular acidosis, a disorder…even with treatment…complicated by osteomalacia with pathologic fractures, hypokalemic muscle weakness and periodic paralysis…eventually leading to death. So we want to believe that his will is more powerful than the…but his body is weak. You may as well face it Bob Cratchet. It's only a matter of time. Your son is dying."

Ebenezer attempted a deep breath, and immediately choked on loose phlegm in his throat, spending much more energy than he wanted dislodging it.

"He's waking," said a voice.

Some moments of shuffling commenced, and he felt a cool damp cloth pat gently across his forehead. His body felt strangely hot and cold all over.

"Jack?" he heard himself muffle.

"Mr. Scrooge? Mr. Scrooge, sir?" Bob's voice was closer. Ebenezer felt a warm hand curl around his own. "What's this about Jack?"

"He must be delusional," Dr. Webber stated.

"I don't think so. 'Jack' is a name we have all heard lately…Some, little boy without a guardian or something."

"I will heat some broth."

"Yes, do that, and bring me my thermometer."

Opening his eyes again, the blur of Bob Cratchet's characteristic fuzzy Irish hair came into view.

"Good morning, Mr. Scrooge. How do you feel?"

Slowly he opened his mouth to speak, feeling an extreme chapped sensation all along his lips, except for the left corner, which felt oddly glued shut. As the moments passed, he began to remember a few more details about the night before. His skin was burned, that much came back right away.

"Where am I?"

"You are in my home, Mr. Scrooge. You will be perfectly safe here."

"Where are Tim and Fred?"

"We still have not found Tim. Fred is out looking."

"Is Tim missing?"

Bob smiled concernedly, and looked over his shoulder, accepting a silver device from someone's hand, and returned.

"Open," Bob said shaking the mercury to the tip of the thermometer.

Ebenezer obeyed sluggishly.

"Good," he said, slipping the cold apparatus into his mouth. He turned again and spoke in soft tones to the other person in the room.

Eyes heavy, Ebenezer moaned.

"Mr. Scrooge," Bob said responding to his every move. "You will need to keep that in your mouth for about twenty minutes."

Bob pulled the watch from his pocket, noting the time, and gave it a good crank before returning it. "I know you need to rest, and I wish you to be well, but I need to ask you some questions. Try not to speak, just nod."

He slowly nodded, despite his throbbing neck.

Bob took in a deep broken breath, and then released it with fenced emotion. "Yes, good. About six hours ago, you came through your office door and murmured something about my son being safe. Do you remember that?"

He shook his head. Even in his drowsy state, the disappointment on Bob's face was evident.

Ebenezer didn't fully understand what was happening, but he sensed that it was urgent. Coming to him in pieces at first, he concentrated and then began remembering the events right before he fell. Reluctantly, he nodded.

"You do? Oh wonderful." Bob smiled. "Eb, do you know where Tim is?" Delivered in desperation, it was the first time Bob Cratchet had *ever* called Mr. Scrooge by a more endearing name.

He pondered the question, as his eyes fell on Bob's intense expression before shaking his head again, only to receive yet another frantic stare.

"Think. Yesterday, we were all at your nephew's house, and when Tim could not be found, you told me that he was in certain danger." Bob gulped and raised his eyebrows in wrinkled arches. "We looked all day, and then…"

Ebenezer tuned him out. Bob continued explaining and moving his arms about, but his thoughts and reflections served to make Bob's words mute.

Suddenly, he *did* remember last night. He remembered the whole day from beginning to end. He had started the morning with fresh burns, and then began a frenzied search for a condemned young Tim who had been chased by a ghost. Later, he discovered it wasn't a ghost at all, and that the young boy that seemed rather normal was actually a spirit…or messenger, as he stated. He even remembered the walk through the colorful halls of memories and glimpses into the future of lives that never were, and yes, even remembered where he had found Tim.

Slowly, he blew against the thermometer, which then slid up and out of his mouth, falling to the pillow against his cheek.

"Help me up," he said weakly.

Bob looked at his acquaintance, which Ebenezer had still not acknowledged, and shrugged. The other man nodded, and then gestured to be very careful.

Instantly, Bob had his hands around Ebenezer's back and shoulder, and tugged ever so slightly, inch by inch, until he was sitting at enough of an angle that he could see the rest of the room. The other man quickly stuffed pillows behind, and Bob delicately released him.

When he was sitting up, and after he had caught his breath, he nodded and sighed.

"Your son was at the chapel."

"But we looked there!"

"Hush. He was in the prayer circle, wallowing in self pity." Breathing heavily, he clenched the muscles in his leg, and released them, thankful that the feeling of his body was waking up again. He was in dire need of rest, and knew it, but it was not hard to guess that he had been in the same exact position on Bob's hard furniture for hours, and it felt good to stretch.

"It is a rather long story, but he is fine. I personally think he is acting like a spoiled child and should be left alone until he comes to his senses, but if you intend to fetch him," he took a deep breath. "Take the dear boy a blanket."

Bob's eyes grew wide, and he leapt from his chair, gripping his black bag, and ran for his coat.

"Dr. Webber, see to Mr. Scrooge! I will return as soon as I can!"

Ebenezer quickly shifted his attention to the other man in the room, realizing he was that doctor from Liverpool. A choleric expression permeated his countenance. The longer he looked at the so called "professional," the more disdain surfaced in Ebenezer's gut, and he turned his gaze back to Bob, awaiting a moment alone with the ignorant fool. If they had been in *his* house instead of Bob's, he would have let Dr. Misdiagnosis have the piece of his mind that he so eagerly anticipated sharing with the man. This was more appealing by far than the ethics of courtesy.

Just as Bob was buttoning his coat, Fred passed by the window, followed by Tim, with what appeared to be a hint more color in his face than he had in the chapel.

Bob rushed to the door with his heart pounding, swung it open, and immediately started unfolding a large heavy blanket.

Fred entered, and stepped aside, allowing Tim to walk past, shutting the door behind them.

"Well, this is very sudden!" Dr. Webber said.

"Indeed," remarked Ebenezer reservedly.

"I was just leaving for the chapel!" Bob shouted.

Fred loosened his scarf. "Yes, that is where I found him. I thought I might check there one more time, and he was there in the middle of the room, sitting on a bench, shivering."

Bob looked through the door.

"Mr. Porter has gone for the women," Fred said, noticing Bob's curiosity. "They will be here soon."

The room was silent. Tim took a deep breath.

"I was in the chapel all night long." Tim began.

Ebenezer nodded, and listened skeptically. Once again, everyone remained still.

"I was in the prayer circle at the foot of the cross."

Bob looked relieved to know his son was alive, but it was evident that he was struggling with hurt, anger, and confusion at realizing he had been intentionally hiding.

"What…" Bob shook his head. "For heaven's sake Tim! What were you *doing* in the chapel all night?"

Tim stepped closer to his father with his head down. "Father, I'm so sorry. I should have come to you." He swallowed hard. "I was facing ghosts of my own…"

For the moment, that answer was to be all he could manage, and with a room full of people and expectations, there didn't seem to be the right platform for a more marvelous explanation. Bob wrapped his son tightly in the blanket, and then hugged him warmly.

"Never do that again, son. NEVER…There's no reason!"

They held each other for a full minute at least. It was like fresh air to Bob's worried soul that he was home safely. Nobody would know the anguish his heart had been through in the last day, or how he prayed silently but constantly that at any given moment he would look up to see Tim at the window again, as he just had.

Fred cleared his throat, and bridled his emotions. Looking at his uncle, he smiled a broken smile, observing the clean gauze dressings around his face.

Dr. Webber was also watching the sad scene of father and son, but his expression was that of even more pain ahead, as if "what a shame" were written in his eyes.

"Listen to me, son," Bob began, gently releasing Tim. "You aren't going anywhere. Do you hear me? You are young, you are healthy, and you have everything to live for. Trust me, you have a long life ahead of you."

Tim nodded as he wiped a few tears off on his blanket.

"I'm sorry, Father."

"And from now on, you *don't* listen to *him*!" Bob pointed angrily at his old medical mentor. Being usually such a meek and soft-spoken man, his demand startled Tim and surprised the rest of the room.

Dr. Webber shook his head hopelessly. "The lad has a right to know the truth."

"There you go again!" Bob exploded.

Tim looked at his father, and then to the older doctor, and smiled confidently. "I do know the truth."

There was a moment of silence, wherein everyone in the room exchanged glances except Dr. Webber and Tim.

"Tim," Dr. Webber said wearily. "You *are* going to die."

Tim stared back, looking assured of himself.

The distinct sound of horses' hooves crumbling fresh snow came from the front lawn. Everyone turned their heads in time to see a carriage driven by Bill Porter containing Anna, little Margaret, Marcus, Emily, and Lillian.

The horses had barely stopped when Anna and the others were scrambling to put their feet on the ground. As expected, Bill remained behind, allowing the family their privacy.

Tim looked at his beautiful, healthy-sized wife struggling to the door through the snow with a baby in her arms. Then he directed his attention back to Dr. Webber, and nodded. "We are *all* going to die someday. However, if you don't mind Dr. Webber, now is just simply not a good time."

At this, Ebenezer laughed out loud. "That's my boy, Tim!" He continued to laugh, which caused a smile to crawl upon Fred's face as well. "Glad to have you back!"

Nobody in the room yet knew what had happened between Ebenezer and Tim only hours before, but just the laughter and verbal confirmation from him of something they didn't yet understand brought them comfort.

The door burst open and Anna threw one arm around her husband and pulled the baby close in a family embrace. He returned her affection wholeheartedly, and kissed her supple lips hard. She pulled away from him, and slapped him across the face severely.

"Mr. Porter told me how Fred found you! Sulking all night like a child while your family doesn't know if you're dead or alive!" Anna broke, burying her face in Tim's blanketed shoulder. "I love you, Tim. I love you…Never disappear on me like this again!" She kissed him a second time.

Shocked, Tim rubbed the sting out of his cheek and creased his forehead.

"I'm…" He couldn't find words. He couldn't fathom how his absence had affected her. This was a side of her he had never seen. "I'm so sorry, Anna. I was scared and foolish. I won't do it again, my love. I promise." It was clear that Tim was beginning to see what Ebenezer meant when he referred to the love of his family.

Emily and Marcus ran in and fell against the knees of their self-adopted big brother.

Lillian had little to say. She smiled warmly, and put her arm around Emily's shoulder. Gazing at the small family, she clasped a thin ivory hand in front of her lips and stammered. "Glad to see you, Tim. Be well."

"Tim! Don't run away ever again!" Emily shouted.

"Yeah Tim," Marcus added sadly. "Why did you go?"

Tim cleared his throat and blinked.

"No, never mind, I don't care why. I'm just glad you're here." Marcus sniffed and wiped the wetness from his face. "Promise me, you won't disappear again."

"Tim," added Emily. "We would never run away from you! So…so…an' please never run away from us!"

Tim lifted his tear-filled eyes to the ceiling and back down. "I promise."

After the children hugged Tim, they slowly approached Ebenezer.

"Uncle," Emily began, smiling at his wrappings. "What game are we playing now?"

"Emily, you nincompoop," Marcus corrected. "This is *not* a game. Uncle Eb has been hurt!"

"You got hurt?" Her eyebrows crunched together concernedly, and her bottom lip puckered. "What happened? Did…an'…did you fall down and break your skin?" Her voice quavered and lifted at the end of her question just before the tears rolled down her bright red cheeks.

"You can't break your skin, silly!" Marcus spat angrily.

In shock, Emily stood speechless, and a moment later, when reality set in, the floodgates of tears broke, and she wailed high-pitched sobs. Instinctively, she reached her arms out to comfort her Uncle Ebby.

"No no no." Fred dashed to intervene.

Holding his hand up to his nephew, Ebenezer smiled gently. "It's alright Fred. Let the little ones come. I could use a hug anyway."

The two children moved closer but didn't expect the bear hug which would be the first of many yet to come.

"Emily my dear," Ebenezer said with a smile. "You must find a way to look on the bright side. Hmm?"

At her great uncle's prompting Emily furrowed her brow in thought, and after tapping her small finger on her chin several times she looked up again.

"Well," she began timidly. "Now when we play our games, you can be REALLY scary now that your face is gross."

"Good gracious!" Lillian cupped her hand over Emily's mouth as her face turned the same shade of scarlet as a ripe cherry.

"Well it's certainly not what I had in mind, but it is indeed a bright side!" Ebenezer exploded into a belly laugh.

Once everyone in the room had seen his reaction, they slowly joined him in his laughter, including Fred who couldn't help but chortle behind his hands.

Eventually, Ebenezer's happy moment lead to a deep chest

cough, which lead to a slight wound reopening at the corner of his mouth.

"Bah, HUMBUG this lip! Bob! The lip!"

Bob immediately turned and accepted his black bag from Dr. Webber and began pilfering through its contents.

After several moments, the commotion had died down, and the room was filled with a peaceful silence. Tim held Anna, and gazed at his lovely baby girl, as Fred, Lillian, Marcus, and Emily all watched Bob gather his supplies. As Bob doctored his friend's mouth, Ebenezer permitted his mind to wander to Melody.

Her sudden appearance in his life had been so short-lived. She spoke her hatred and regret so openly, and when it was over, it felt as surreal as a dream.

He *would* fulfill his promise.

"There you are Mr. Scrooge," Bob said dabbing lightly.

Still in thought, Ebenezer's eyes met a nearby vacant chair.

"…though you will not see me, until then, I will be in every empty chair beside you…"

Jack's echoing words brought a lump to Ebenezer's throat, and a smile to his face. He looked at Fred. "Fred, my dear, sweet nephew, Merry Christmas. Instead of a gift this year, I give you a burden."

"Uncle?" Fred asked confused.

"I would like to relocate myself immediately…if your offer still stands?"

CHAPTER TWENTY-ONE

Three Years Later

Tim stared down at his fingertips and marveled at the amount of ink that had never even made it to the parchment. The quill's plain brown feather was even inked several inches above his hand, and it didn't feel like an inanimate object anymore, but rather functioned like a natural extension of his body. The small sample of writing that he had now tasted, tempered by the time in Ebenezer's office, had matured his writing passion to the point that there was no need to contemplate physically making the words appear on the parchment anymore. It was as natural as breathing.

Leaning back in his chair, he sighed deeply and reflected warmly on the task that was now complete. He was sure that his accomplishment would make his father and Ebenezer happy. Now the world would know the story about the old miser who had changed his ways that fateful Christmas Eve with the help of three ghostly visitors.

Blinking, he contemplated continuing the story from there…

Should he?

Should he write about what happened sixteen years later when Ebenezer was visited by a strange boy named Jack?

Should he include his own personal descent into a pit of depression where he almost gave up on life?

Perhaps he could consider sharing with the world about how

Ebenezer felt trapped in his own city because of his legendary appeal after he turned over his new leaf?

No...That was a story for someone else to write, someday. For now, this would be where the story ended.

Smiling, he closed his eyes and thought. This book, assuming it would be published, would be the splendid icing on the most scrumptious of all life's cakes. Everything had gone perfect lately.

With that in mind, there was one thing he wanted to do before too much time had gone by, and before he was at risk of forgetting important details. In moments, his inkwell was pulled close to a leather-bound book with empty pages, and his ink splattered fingertips were pinching the tip of his quill once more. This journal entry would be the first of many that would record so many of life's miracles and joys...

To my children, and their children after that:

I have just completed the first of many books that I intend to publish. I feel the need to share a few intimate details of my life and times with those closest to me that the readers of my novels will never know.

The following writings will be with me until I am gone, so while you read this, remember me well, and as you think on my memory, please consider those who have made me what I am and who you remember me to be. I want you to think on them as well.

Tim thought about where to begin...

Just three years ago, I felt lost and forsaken by the terrible circumstance of an improper diagnosis from a "Dr. Webber," of whom by now you have surely heard. To think of all I would have lost if I had truly believed I was in for death, and given up on life! I cannot imagine.

However, Dr. Webber has always been a brilliant doctor, who has taught Bob Cratchet, my father, your grandfather (or great-grandfather, as it may be), so many things. It is for this fact that I still greatly respect him. His most recent development makes me laugh out loud when I think of it even now!

My father and Dr. Webber have decided to live past their differences. About three years ago, they announced that they were to open a medical office together. Dr. Webber was getting older, (you see, his years were numbered), and he wanted to leave his legacy in the hands of someone he could trust, and who better than your grandfather? With a little financial help from Mr. Scrooge, the newly formed practice was up and running within the year.

Not long thereafter, Dr. Webber offered an exciting suggestion to my father as an alternative for the lonely time he spent away from the office. (His wife, my mother, Margaret, had passed away, and his children were all grown. His practice was all he had, and this made him feel lonely.) The suggestion inspired Father to make arrangements right away. He created his own medical school right there in the back of their building! People came (and still come!) from miles around to learn from "Tiny Tim's" own father, and the graduates were eventually learned enough to see to the patients while my father was busy teaching. Oh what an arrangement it was!

Dr. Webber retired shortly after the school began its unavoidable success, and decided he would write one more book to add to his collection of medical curriculum. Many years after he is gone, he will be most remembered for the final, but most effective, remedy based on the witnessed events of my own personal recovery, *The Power of the Will to Live: Medicine of a Miracle*, which he wrote in only six months.

Tim paused, and ran the clean end of his quill across his cheek in thought.

Yes, many things had happened in the last three years, and with the family he loved. His wonderful family…

Marcus and Emily were best friends half the time, and worst enemies the other half.

Marcus had developed an unusual hobby of crafting miniature plays from his game ideas, and Ebenezer would assist in writing them down.

"I tell you m'boy, with that imagination, you are sure to be a better playwright than the great Shakespeare himself!" he would say.

Emily had become quite the guest entertainer, pretending to cook lavish seven-course meals, scheduling tea parties with the grown-ups, all the while learning to crochet a perfect doily.

Little Margaret could run with excellent balance, speak with a five-year-old's vocabulary, and had many similarities to her mother just before her third birthday. With her unpolished charisma and innocent shamelessness, she stole the hearts of everyone that knew her, and had established the nickname "Cheeky."

Anna had become even more plump than she was when they had married, and was all the happier for it, saying there was more of her to love. This comment about her own figure said in public undoubtedly caused several other women to frown on her "vulgarity." She decided it would be best not to attempt bringing their attention to the level of destruction their own vulgar gossip had caused others. This peaceful reaction earned her a great deal of respect from several observers, which resulted in pathetic jealousy from the petty women who originally intended to elevate their own status at her expense.

Tim smiled, proud of his wife's discernment. He was proud of his whole family, Ebenezer included.

He laughed out loud, and dipped his quill again.

During this time, Ebenezer (I hope, for your sake, he lives long enough for you to meet him, for he is indeed a merry soul!), conceded finally, and moved in with his family. Fred and Lillian absolutely adored the addition of Ebenezer to their home. It was by all means large enough to invite him in comfortably. Even though he left most of his things behind for the time being, he still found his nephew's house much cozier.

At first, Fred's family was restless, staying up all throughout the night and straining to hear if their uncle was safely in bed or not, which was easier to do from down the hall than across London, where he lived before. You see, Ebenezer had terrible dreams, and while he lived alone, everyone worried, as the dreams often lead to an injury. Oh how that man would toss in his bed! Eventually however, about three months into his new life without a single nightmare, Fred and his family finally began to rest, and when they did, it was the best rest they had gotten in a little over sixteen years! They even learned that they enjoyed sleeping in late almost every day, awakening to the smell of bacon and eggs, and a happily whistled tune flowing from the kitchen.

If only you could have been there—

In all of Fred's life, and even after his uncle had changed, he had to *see* it to believe that Ebenezer would ever don an apron and make an early breakfast. It even made it worth hearing the fussing and grumbling that would often be heard after the coffee was spilled or an egg didn't crack properly. But the old merry soul, he was his old grumpy self, and his constant protests of low quality eggshells and malfunctioning imported French percolators were music to their ears!

I'm sure you are curious how a man can be called "merry" and "grumpy" in the same letter (or the same sentence for that matter!), but to describe a man like Mr. Ebenezer Scrooge places the writer in the position to abandon all grammatical standards, as he is all by himself, an anomaly. He is indeed the most interesting of personalities!

Tim thought back on these happy moments, and felt very grateful that everyone was still alive and healthy for now. He had learned to cherish every moment that they had to live.

Thinking back, Ebenezer had almost left their happy little group a few times…

Tim was sure that Ebenezer's burns were by far the most painful wounds a man could endure. His burns took a very long time to heal.

The way he suffered…

Reflecting on the time that followed Ebenezer's fireside slumber, Tim remembered how his old friend had undergone some very painful healing. His skin could not be open to the fresh air for fear of the high risk of infection. He couldn't remain covered for long with the same gauze without it attaching to the wounds. So three or four times a day, for weeks, he sat patiently while Bob gently removed his wrappings and reapplied them, braving a constant removal of dead skin and exposure of the tender under-flesh. Bob openly admitted that the old griping miser was one of the toughest men he had ever seen. Of course, Bob was the first to be lashed out at every time something unexpectedly painful happened, but for the sake of truly gold-hearted Mr. Scrooge, he didn't mind at all.

Eventually, the healing process drew to a long awaited and very refreshing end.

Once completely healed however, Ebenezer was still terribly disfigured. Having remained indoors while his wounds were fresh to avoid the harmful rays of the sun and germs in the air, he had not been seen in public since the day after the accident. For the sake of unwanted charity and gossip, those closest to him decided to keep quiet about his injuries, and let everyone in the surrounding cities and towns draw their own conclusions. They agreed that if and when Ebenezer decided to rejoin the public, they would all address those issues later. Everyone regarded him mournfully the morning he pulled on his coat and decided it was "now or never ol' Scrooge m'boy," because living in fear of people's judgment was a humbug.

Nobody expected to see a giddy old man racing through the door in a fit of laughter several hours later.

"They didn't know it was me!" he was shouting.

"I stopped just outside the office, and heard two ladies speak about my mysterious disappearance, and one woman said to the other, she said, she said, 'Amazing isn't it? No trace of him anywhere; he's just up and gone.' And the other one," he continued, speaking a million words a minute, "she said, she said, 'I heard he died.' Hee heeee! I'm free! I'm a free man!"

A little shocked at first and very confused, Fred, Bob, and the children followed Ebenezer into the study, where he right away demand that champagne be brought for the celebration of the great news. When everyone stood dumbfounded and staring, he started laughing again and gestured for everyone to sit. He then launched into several short stories of his afternoon out. He had flat out spoken face-to-face with shop owners that he had seen every day for years, and they regarded him as a poor misshapen beggar, one even offered him a free piece of bread because he looked hungry.

One person in the shopping district *did* recognize him, and, at Ebenezer's request, promised not to tell a soul.

Because of that promise, Bill Porter became his personal assistant for the new plans Ebenezer had made.

Mr. Porter would go to town, on behalf of "an unsociable friend," and conduct all of Ebenezer's business matters, with full access to all his monies to distribute accordingly.

First Tim headed to town and offered ownership of the land to every one of Mr. Scrooge's tenants, at a price they could easily afford and therefore would not refuse. Mr. Porter helped Tim in handling all the legalities. Then, Ebenezer opened a place for widows and orphans or people needing to escape rough situations, in a secluded and secret location that appeared abandoned to ensure their safety. They were welcome to stay there for as long as it took them to get back on their feet or make other arrangements. The establishment was guarded, and all communication from the outside world was monitored. Once a person was ready to leave, they were properly escorted to a safe area.

That he knew of, no place like this had ever been instituted in London, and after Ebenezer's brief meeting with Melody, he simply couldn't ignore the need for such a site. When he spoke in secret with his family and Bill Porter about this place, he referred to it as the "Belle Memorial Safe House." This wonderful place had been founded and set up immediately after one promise had been tended to…

It only took one afternoon to set Bill up with his own office, away from the suspicious location of Mr. Scrooge's old building. His son was more than delighted to permanently take over "Porter's

Dresses, Hats, and Jewelry." Bill's first assignment was to buy a piece of land with a move-in-ready home. Mr. Scrooge's personal house would not do at all, as it was a renowned location by this time, and it was in everyone's interest that the location be discreet. Within one week, professionals were hired, and within three weeks from that point, Belle's children had been found. Apparently, they were living in the streets, doing the unthinkable for money. There were no living relatives in the Fezziwig family that would even acknowledge them. Once Belle's father and mother, the loving, kindhearted, and respectful leaders of the family had passed away, the rest of them turned up their noses to Belle and her offspring, acting ashamed of whom she had married. His behavior was apparently so disgraceful, that the Fezziwig's could not consider him as a separate entity to their own flesh and blood, even when they were most in need. The thought of reputation succeeding the importance of a human life was positively evil in Ebenezer's eyes. However, rather than confront them or judge them for committing the same inhumane acts that he himself had been guilty of in years past, he would intervene quietly.

Tim himself and Mr. Porter were to see to the discreet project with him. Knowing just where the children were seen last, they had no trouble finding them again.

Tim saw the look on Melody's face when the modest wooden carriage, enclosed by a curtain and driven by Bill and Tim, pulled up and stopped alongside the brick sidewalk. She was standing there with her head down in her quintessential purple cloak. When she finally looked up, she had the appearance of one who expected to be accused of something.

Later, when they regaled Ebenezer with the specifics of what happened outside the curtain, they said that the woman was ready to run when Bill first handed her the folded parchment. She approached him skeptically. Then jerking it out of his hand, she backed up several steps, looked up the street, and then down, and slowly lowered her eyes. She closely studied the wax seal that read "ES" in beautiful letters, and "To Melody" written just below.

Tim smiled, remembering the way she had looked at her hands for a full minute or so before finally peeling back the wax and opening the note. Upon seeing an empty page, save for the words "I told you I would come," she looked back up in shock, and shook her head. Her eyes quickly darted from Bill who was a few steps away from her on the ground, then to Tim who was behind the reigns, and then to the curtain.

Tim had told Ebenezer many times how her expression had evolved while she stood staring at the carriage.

"It was as if she was shocked at first," Tim had said. "Then she almost looked afraid, almost expecting it to be a trap of some sort. Many times she looked up and down the street. I haven't the slightest idea why, unless she perhaps suspected we hadn't come alone. Maybe she was considering calling for help, though I can't imagine anyone being afraid of *us*. I just remember that between my limp and Bill's timid nature, we wouldn't have tried to catch her if she ran, so I just continued to pray in my head that she would trust us long enough to receive what you had for her." Tim had slapped his knee as he would tell the story, loving this part the best. "I remember how she eventually tilted her chin up, straightened her cloak, and walked very slowly to the carriage."

That was a day that none of the three men would forget…

"What do you want?" Melody's beautiful eyes were narrowed to hateful slits. She sat stiff and rigid on the carriage seat with her arms folded across her chest and her hood down.

Ebenezer tried not to focus on her appearance, but it was hard not to notice that her face, hair, and clothing were far dirtier than the day they met in the alleyway. However, he was glad that they had at least gotten past the detailed explanation of his appearance. Their last meeting didn't offer any props for addressing that issue at length.

"I have something for you." It was a larger envelope, but this time did not bear his own seal.

"What is it?"

"A very tardy gift that I give you free and clear, to share with your brothers."

She made no move to take it from him, and instead moved her gaze to the curtain that separated her and Ebenezer from Bill and Tim. She was sure that they could hear everything, and felt the need to be ready to jump from the carriage at any sign of movement. The very thought of it made her unfold her arms and curl her fingers around the edge of the seat in preparation for a getaway.

"Dear lady," Ebenezer continued.

She looked back.

"It is only an envelope. Not poison." His sincere smile was sweet and encouraging.

"What is *inside* your non-poisonous envelope?" she sneered.

He thought for a moment about the contents, and the deed to such an extravagant home and land paid in full. He feared that if she opened it in front of him, that her pride would not allow her to accept the gift.

"You will see what is inside when you decide to open it. I will leave it with you, and you can inspect it upon your own convenience."

Tim recalled the way she looked as they drove away. Standing in the middle of the street holding an oversized white envelope, the wind had picked up just enough to cause a faint ripple at the bottom of her cloak as she faded from view.

He considered including this event in his journal entry.

No...It wasn't his memory to tell. That should remain between Ebenezer and Melody.

Ebenezer felt greatly blessed when a letter arrived a few months later. He opened it eagerly.

Dearest Mr. Ebenezer Scrooge,

We are safe.

We are grateful.

You know where we live.

DO drop by for a visit—soon.

The letter wasn't even signed. It didn't need to be.

He showed the letter to Tim and Mr. Porter proudly.

Choking up, remembering the paramount importance that this letter had on Ebenezer, Tim cleared his throat, and dipped his quill.

Yes, our friend Ebenezer is quite a man, of which there is no equal.

By the time you read this, you will no doubt have been told about his final years on earth. You will likely have made the connection between "The Faceless Beggar" and the famous Mr. Scrooge. I hope someday your mothers and fathers will tell you the stories, and continue to pass them down, of the wonders he did in disguise. If you haven't heard, (scold your parents on my behalf, and then read on!) here is the story, just as it happened:

After the burns, Ebenezer continued to revel in his secret. Before long, he had developed his own identity throughout the town as "The Faceless Beggar." People continued to stare and point, but his true self was now masked forever, and privacy was now his to keep.

Once in a while, he would call for Mr. Porter. (Mr. Porter was another jolly soul. You would have liked him, as everyone did.)

"Bill," he would say. "I overheard last night that so-and-so's horse passed away. Leave a colt on their doorstep with a ribbon 'round its neck."

Then he would laugh, and slap his knee, and plan for his next anonymous good deed.

Oh how he had begun to really, thoroughly enjoy life, like he never had before!

A while later, one of the most enjoyable events of his life transpired. It was not as if Mr. Scrooge's funds were running low, but he wanted the things that he had overseen during his lifetime to continue and prosper even after he was gone.

After several days of brainstorming, he finally had an idea.

Ah yes, I remember the very look on his face, and the shaking of his arms when he bolted from the study, with wine spilt on his shirt, shouting, "I did it! I did it! I know what to do!"

He had everyone's attention immediately. In addition to having formed a trust fund, another more novel self-perpetuating income idea for after he was gone had surfaced. He told his family, along with your Grandfather Cratchet, Mr. Porter and me of his plans, and received unanimously positive feedback.

So, as was always the way with Mr. Scrooge, plans started at once!

One month later, the "Ebenezer Scrooge Museum" opened for business.

In addition to a tour of the inside of his own personal home, a gift shop was assembled in the attic where people could purchase the "Ghost Set" of four ceramic statuettes depicting Jacob Marley alongside the Ghosts of Christmas Past, Present, and Future, among other novelties. Mr. Porter might not have been good at selling hats, but his ideas behind the scenes at the museum were brilliant!

On opening day, the museum made more money than the office did in a month, and included cameo appearances by Bob Cratchet, Timothy Cratchet, and unbeknownst to all, in the back of the tour, "The Faceless Beggar." Oh how he beamed!

He had later told his family and your Grandfather Cratchet and me in confidence that he had to bite his lip during the entire event to keep himself from adding to the tour guide's list of things to say. It was especially difficult for him to remain quiet when the guide forgot to mention how the door glowed terribly bright at the hour of two o'clock, when the Ghost of Christmas Present appeared behind it.

His favorite part of the tour was when someone from downstairs pulled the bell chains at the exact moment the tour approached them, in an attempt to reenact their ringing by themselves right before the sinister Jacob Marley floated in.

Oh-ho! It was a wonderful dramatization of the entire event!

People traveled far and wide to be so close to the famous Mr. Scrooge's home, bed, hall, fireplace, office, and safe, and even in those hard times, continued to pay nearly any ticket price asked of them. The demand for the handmade gift shop items and locally brewed refreshments, in addition to the foot traffic, eventually resulted in the collaboration of the locals, driving all of Ebenezer's old tenants' businesses through the roof!

London had their celebrity.

Mr. Scrooge had his anonymity.

Tim tilted forward again in his chair.

That was exactly why the story had to be told, and *now*.

From what Ebenezer and his father had told him, he was the only one who could write the story for it to be published with such extreme success…

"It must be written by your hand, and your hand alone Tim."

"But Ebenezer, I'm not a writer! I'm a scribe!"

He remembered the look in Ebenezer's eyes.

"I know how you feel, and I hate to put such a burden on you, but you are the only one who can. Trust me, it is what Jack said must happen."

Even Tim couldn't argue against the word of "Jack." Turning his attention to the top of the bookshelf to his left, he smiled, remembering the stories surrounding the boy. He was glad that Ebenezer had that silly little clicking spoon toy stored in a custom glass case for preservation. The quill certainly wasn't going to last very long at this rate…

I am sure that by now you have been told about the small boy named Jack. (Hopefully you are old enough that you were able to sit in on one of Ebenezer's personal storytellings for this particular boy!) It is important that you know who he is. He played a great role in changing all of our lives for the better. Do you remember the story of how I disappeared for a short time overnight in a chapel?

I recall my return from the chapel that Christmas

morning. My father demanded my attention, alone. I will tell you of that conversation now.

"There is something I should have told you a long time ago, son," my father said.

"You…" He put his hands on my shoulders while he spoke, and looked at me squarely. I will never forget it. "You were stillborn."

I felt faint! I don't remember how I reacted, other than to tell you that when the truth of what he said had hit me, my father had to hold me steady.

"What? You mean…born dead?" I asked.

Father nodded and pointed upward. Then he said, "Somebody up there has a big plan for you. When your mother went into labor with you, I could not be there because Mr. Scrooge would not let me leave the office. When I arrived, you looked normal and healthy. Granted, you were small, but everything seemed normal."

I stared at him in disbelief, (as anyone would!) and looked down at the ground. I remember I shook my head, unable to grasp what was happening. Of course, your grandfather, being the kind of man he was, knew that it was best to continue.

"Your mother forgave me for having been too late to witness your coming into the world, and about three months later, she told me something very strange," he said. At this point, I had to fight the urge to pass out. I couldn't allow myself to miss out on a thing!

So he continued on. "She said that she was in our living room, writing me a note, when the front door opened. She looked up from the table, and a small boy was suddenly standing there. He told her very candidly that the baby inside her was dead, but he would soon be alive again, and she needed to do whatever possible to protect that child."

Of course I said the only thing I could think of to say at the time.

"Who was...Who was he?" I asked. "Is that...Is that why mother died...while I was sick? She—protected—me—even to her own death?"

When I had started to sob, father hugged me close and allowed me to cry. Sometimes it seems like the world will never stop mourning the loss of my sweet mother. I had spent years blaming myself for her death and the last thing I needed at that moment was confirmation that it was my fault.

I felt helpless. Of course once again the only thing that Father could think of to do was just keep talking. What would you have done?

So the next thing he said was how the boy simply waved, smiled, and left the way he came in. The second the door closed behind him, my mother went into a very painful labor. She had told Father that the whole appearance of the boy was very strange, and she was restless for weeks.

Then, he came back to her.

"What happened then?" you ask.

According to my mother's words, he appeared next to the bassinet one day and remarked how delightful I looked, as a baby, lying there. When my mother reached in to try to take me away, she said the boy just smiled, and told her not to be afraid, because he was just a little boy, and little boys aren't scary.

I was confused and shocked by the mention of this mysterious boy.

He then told her that I was made for a special reason,

and that his Boss was the only one who knew what that was. She asked him for whom he worked, and the boy didn't answer. He reached under his hat, and pulled out a feather.

"A feather?" I asked Father, as I was terribly confused.

Father nodded.

"Yes. I didn't know what it meant any more than she did, but I have it here with me."

I asked him then, if the little boy said anything else.

"Yes," Father said, and then reached into his dress coat pocket. "He gave your mother the feather, and told her to remember the words, 'take up the quill,' so you would know someday."

"So *I* would know?" I asked bewildered.

Father nodded again.

I asked, "So I would know *what*? What am I supposed to know?"

Father shrugged sadly and shook his head. "I have told you all I know." He slipped the feather, along with an old, faded letter into my fingertips, and held me again. Later, when I read the letter, it confirmed everything Father had told me.

It was only later that day that Ebenezer told me and Father his entire story in detail from the moment he met Jack. There was no doubt in our minds that the mysterious little boy was one and the same.

This is why I write.

Tim decided to stop for the time being. He could always resume later, but for now, his hand had been cramping for days.

He was proud of himself now, looking down at the finished manuscript and the new journal.

"Here you are, mother," he said with a reminiscent smile.

Tim, still fumbling with the inky quill in his fingers, pulled it closer to his face, and examined it.

"May every man's guardian angel haunt him to redemption."

Such a plain feather to be left from such an important character. In the light of eternity, any primary feather is a feather that will make a good quill either way, but it was unique and humble of "Little Jack, the Messenger" to leave an ordinary brown feather, instead of a big, frilly, snow-white one.

Tim himself preferred the plain, thin brown feather. It reminded him of himself.

"Alright ol' boy!" he said, settling the quill back in its resting place. "The ending sounds like a good place to stop..."

But is it ever really the end?

He stood from his leather chair, and stretched his arms high, releasing a shudder. His long, lanky body now almost identically resembled his father's, with the exception of his slightly crooked leg.

Someone was approaching the window. Tim had been concentrating for so long on his parchment, he didn't even attempt to focus until the person got much closer.

Moments later, a widespread grin appeared on Tim's face, and he limped toward the door to let his best friend in.

"Ahhh! Good day to you, Mr. Cratchet!" Ebenezer said smiling.

"Yes, and to *you*, Old Beggar! Come inside! See my newly arranged office! Let me get you something to eat! You're skinny as a rail!"

"And twice as pale?" Ebenezer quipped.

"Ha ha, of course!"

Tim welcomed his now slow-moving companion inside, and closed the door behind him.

"What do you think?" Tim asked.

Ebenezer looked around in awe, and laughed.

"It looks a great deal more comfortable than it did when we ran it together, doesn't it?"

Tim chuckled, and nodded.

"It will do for a writer." He gestured for Ebenezer to sit.

"Oh no, I mustn't! I have an engagement."

"Oh?" Tim said with excitement. "Where are you off to?"

"The carriage is meeting me in two hours just outside the train station." He looked happy, but nervous. "I have decided it's time."

Tim clapped once ecstatically, and hugged the old hunchback.

"Glad to hear it!"

"I want to tell them all about their mother, and the woman she was back in the days when I was idiot enough to let her go."

"Don't be nervous old man," Tim teased.

"I will be whatever I darn well choose to be!" He paused. "Is it obvious?"

"You're shaking like a leaf, Ebenezer."

"Well, I don't care! It's now or never, and I'm going through with it this time. They deserve to hear about their mother before everything went wrong, and they deserve to hear it from the horse's mouth." He pointed his finger at himself decidedly.

"I always thought you to be a horse," Tim added with a laugh.

"Quiet you!" Ebenezer grinned, and poked Tim's belly with the cane.

Tim smiled at his old friend for several uninterrupted seconds, finally deciding it was best *not* to tell the old man about the rumor that Melody had lied, and Belle was alive and staying with her children. If it ended up false, it would break his heart. If it were true, he would never gain the courage to climb into that carriage. Besides, it seemed silly to even bring up something that was said by Bill, who heard from an old woman, who heard it from a man, who used to know the Fezziwig family…

"Oh yes," Ebenezer said, interrupting Tim's thought. "One more thing. How is my story coming along?"

"Well," Tim answered, trying to appear nonchalant about his thoughts. "I only have one thing to do before I'm finished."

"What!?" Ebenezer's melted face exploded with urgency.

"I have to sign it."

"What are you standing around for, looking like a right ninny? Sign it!"

"Well Ebenezer," Tim paced, tapping his finger on his lip thoughtfully. "If I have learned anything from you, it is the value of anonymity."

"Oh? You need a false name?"

"Yes, and preferably one that sounds incredibly dignified…" He stopped pacing and looked at the old man.

"I think I rather fancy the name 'Charles Dickens.' What do you think?"